The Protection of Cultural Heritage During Armed Conflict

This book analyses the current legal framework seeking to protect cultural heritage during armed conflict and discusses proposed and emerging paradigms for its better protection. Cultural heritage has always been a victim of conflict, with monuments and artefacts frequently destroyed as collateral damage in wars throughout history. In addition, works of art have been viewed as booty by victors and stolen in the aftermath of conflict. However, deliberate destruction of cultural sites and items has also occurred, and the intentional destruction of cultural heritage has been a hallmark of recent conflicts in the Middle East and North Africa, where we have witnessed unprecedented, systematic attacks on culture as a weapon of war. In Iraq, Syria, Libya, Yemen, and Mali, extremist groups such as ISIS and Ansar Dine have committed numerous acts of iconoclasm, deliberately destroying heritage sites and looting valuable artefacts symbolic of minority cultures. This study explores how the international law framework can be fully utilised in order to tackle the destruction of cultural heritage, and analyses various paradigms which have recently been suggested for its better protection, including the Responsibility to Protect paradigm and the peace and security paradigm.

This volume will be an essential resource for scholars and practitioners in the areas of public international law, especially international humanitarian law and cultural heritage law.

Noelle Higgins is an Associate Professor of Law at Maynooth University Department of Law, Ireland.

The Protection of Cultural Heritage During Armed Conflict
The Changing Paradigms

Noelle Higgins

LONDON AND NEW YORK

First published 2020 by Routledge
2 Park Square, Milton Park, Abingdon, Oxon OX14 4RN

and by Routledge
605 Third Avenue, New York, NY 10017

First issued in paperback 2021

Routledge is an imprint of the Taylor & Francis Group, an informa business

Copyright © 2020 Noelle Higgins

The right of Noelle Higgins to be identified as authors of this work has been asserted by them in accordance with sections 77 and 78 of the Copyright, Designs and Patents Act 1988.

All rights reserved. No part of this book may be reprinted or reproduced or utilised in any form or by any electronic, mechanical, or other means, now known or hereafter invented, including photocopying and recording, or in any information storage or retrieval system, without permission in writing from the publishers.

Trademark notice: Product or corporate names may be trademarks or registered trademarks, and are used only for identification and explanation without intent to infringe.

Publisher's Note
The publisher has gone to great lengths to ensure the quality of this reprint but points out that some imperfections in the original copies may be apparent.

British Library Cataloguing-in-Publication Data
A catalogue record for this book is available from the British Library

Library of Congress Cataloging-in-Publication Data
A catalog record has been requested for this book

ISBN 13: 978-1-03-223614-8 (pbk)
ISBN 13: 978-0-367-25391-2 (hbk)

Typeset in Times New Roman
by Deanta Global Publishing Services, Chennai, India

Contents

Acknowledgements vii

Introduction 1

Introductory comments 1
What is cultural heritage? 6
Research question 7
Structure 7

1 Traditional paradigms on the protection of cultural heritage during armed conflict 8

Introduction 8
The legal framework protecting cultural heritage 10
   'Civilian use' and 'culture-value' paradigms on the protection of cultural heritage 19
   Human rights and cultural rights 19
   Customary international law 21
Individual criminal responsibility for crimes against culture and the international criminal law jurisprudence 22
   Individual criminal responsibility 22
   The ICTY and the destruction of cultural heritage 25
The ICC and the Al Mahdi *case 27*
Conclusion 34

2 Potential paradigms: Cultural cleansing, the Responsibility to Protect doctrine and cultural genocide 36

Introduction 36
What is 'cultural cleansing'? 38
The R2P doctrine 39
    The development of the R2P doctrine 39
    The R2P doctrine and the protection of cultural heritage 43
Cultural genocide 47
    The conceptualisation of genocide 48
    Genocide as an international crime 50
    Cultural genocide and indigenous peoples 55
Conclusion 58

3 The securitisation of cultural heritage 60

Introduction 60
UN resolutions on cultural heritage 63
    The destruction of cultural heritage as a peace and security issue in UN resolutions 65
    UN Security Council Resolution 2347 (2017) 65
    Success of Resolution 2347 70
Cultural Peacekeeping 72
UNESCO initiatives 81
Peacebuilding and sustainable development 83
Conclusion 84

Conclusion 87
Bibliography 93
Index 104

Acknowledgements

Some of the work for this book was undertaken during a research visit to the Asia-Pacific Centre for Military Law at Melbourne Law School, and I am extremely grateful for the support of the Law School, especially of Prof Alison Duxbury, who facilitated my visit, and of Dr Emma Nyhan. I would like to sincerely thank my students, and my extensive support network at home and abroad, as well as to all the team at Routledge for their contributions to the final product.

Rinne mé roinnt oibre don leabhar seo agus mé ar chuairt taighde san Asia-Pacific Centre for Military Law ag Scoil Dlí Melbourne, agus táim fíor-bhuíoch as tacaíocht na Scoile, go háirithe as an tacaíocht a fuair mé ón Ollamh Alison Duxbury, a d'éascaigh an chuairt, agus ón Dr Emma Nyhan. Ba mhaith liom buíochas ó chroí a ghabháil le mo chuid mac léinn agus le mo lucht tacaíochta i bhfad agus i gcéin, chomh maith le foireann Routledge, a chuir go mór leis an táirge deiridh.

Introduction

Introductory comments

Cultural heritage has always been a victim of conflict, with monuments and artefacts being frequently destroyed as collateral damage in wars throughout history.[1] In addition, works of art have been viewed as booty by victors and stolen in the aftermath of conflict.[2] However, deliberate destruction of cultural sites and items has also occurred. In the post-Cold War era, for example, we witnessed deliberate targeting of cultural heritage in identity wars in places such as the former Yugoslavia.[3] Intentional destruction of cultural heritage is also a hallmark of more recent conflicts in the Middle East and North Africa, where we have seen unprecedented, systematic attacks on culture as a weapon of war. In Iraq, Syria, Libya, Yemen, and Mali, extremist groups such as the Islamic State of Iraq and Syria (ISIS) and Ansar Dine have committed numerous acts of iconoclasm, deliberately destroying heritage sites and looting valuable artefacts symbolic of minority cultures. This destruction of cultural heritage has been described as 'cultural cleansing' by the former director-general of the United Nations Educational, Scientific and Cultural Organization (UNESCO).[4] This label illustrates that fundamentalist Islamic groups aim to

---

1 See Francesco Francioni and Federico Lenzerini, 'The Obligation to Prevent and Avoid Destruction of Cultural Heritage: From Bamiyan to Iraq', in Barbara T. Hoffman (ed) Art and Cultural Heritage (Cambridge University Press 2006), 28.
2 See Jiri Toman, *The Protection of Cultural Property in the Event of Armed Conflict* (Dartmouth Publishing Company 1996), 3. See also Roger O'Keefe, *The Protection of Cultural Property during Armed Conflict* (Cambridge University Press 2006).
3 See Helen Walasek et al., *Bosnia and the Destruction of Cultural Heritage* (Routledge 2016). See also Hirad Abtathi, 'The Protection of Cultural Property in Times of Armed Conflict: The Practice of the International Criminal Tribunal for the Former Yugoslavia' (2001) 14 *Harvard Human Rights Journal* 1; Theodor Meron, 'The Protection of Cultural Property in the Event of Armed Conflict within the Case-law of the International Criminal Tribunal for the Former Yugoslavia' (2005) 57(4) *Museum International* 41.
4 See Irina Bokova, 'Culture on the Front Line of New Wars' (2015) 22 *Brown Journal of World Affairs* 289, 289.

2 Introduction

eradicate all signs of cultures different from their own and purify the area of cultural representations of 'the Other.'[5] The recent attacks aimed to eliminate diversity and pluralism, to 'erase all sources of belonging and identity, and destroy the fabric of society.'[6] Foradori and Rosa comment that '[b]y obliterating the memory of the past (*damnatio memoriae*), ISIS wants to re-set and re-write history with a new beginning, a "year zero" as of which only its own vision of the world is entitled to exist.'[7] These attacks have also led to the displacement of peoples and groups, and thus have contributed to the dilution or erosion of their cultural heritage and expressions. The consequences for individuals' lives, for group identity, and for the societies in these States have been deep and will persist long after the conflicts end.[8] A UNESCO report states that

---

5 Bokova states that 'Cultural cleansing is a tactic of war, used to destabilize populations and weaken social defences. The destruction of heritage undermines wellsprings of identity and belonging, paving the way to social disintegration. Eliminating layers of history, cities and homes affects people's perception of the past and present and shadows their confidence in a future where their rights and dignity would be respected.' See ibid., p. 291. Regarding attacks on 'the Other,' see Jadranka Petrovic, 'The Cultural Dimension of Peace Operations: Peacekeeping and Cultural Property', in Andrew H Campbell (ed), *Global Leadership Initiatives for Conflict Resolution and Peacebuilding* (IGI Global 2018), 84, 84. See also, UNESCO, 'Background Note to the International Conference "Heritage and Cultural Diversity at Risk in Iraq and Syria" – The Protection of Heritage and Cultural Diversity: A Humanitarian and Security Imperative in the Conflicts of the 21st Century', UNESCO Headquarters, Paris (3 December 2014), 1–2, which states that 'cultural cleansing ... seeks to destroy the legitimacy of the "other" to exist as such. Through the deliberate targeting of minorities, schools, cultural heritage sites and property, the foundations of society are undermined in a durable manner and social fragmentation accelerated. These attacks are often compounded by the looting and illicit trafficking of cultural objects, which contribute to global organized crime and, in turn, to fuelling armed conflict. In this context, protecting cultural heritage and integrating the cultural dimension in conflict prevent and resolution constitutes more than a cultural emergency – it is a political, humanitarian and security imperative.'
6 Irina Bokova, 'Culture on the Front Line of New Wars' (2015) 22 *Brown Journal of World Affairs* 289, 290.
7 Paolo Foradori and Paolo Rosa, 'Expanding the Peacekeeping Agenda. The Protection of Cultural Heritage in War-Torn Societies' (2017) 29(2) *Global Change, Peace and Security* 145, 150.
8 Ibid. Concerning the more recent attacks on cultural heritage, Foradori and Rosa state: 'This escalation is to a large extent connected to the changing nature of warfare and in particular the emergence in the post-Cold War security environment of what have been termed "new wars" or "contemporary conflicts" ... the *politics of identity* are at the heart of these conflicts, and religious and ethnic dimensions are key features defining the motivations and the objectives of contemporary warfare. Identity is largely shaped and influenced by culture; if cultural property visualizes identity, it is not surprising that cultural heritage has become a direct and deliberate target of warfare in recent and current conflicts.'

[t]he forced displacements in both Iraq and Syria are threatening to cause an irreversible modification of these country's [sic.] social fabric and cohesion, with far-reaching consequences not only for their rich cultural diversity but also for stability in the region and national reconciliation.[9]

John Kerry, US Secretary of State, described the destruction of cultural heritage in Syria as 'a purposeful final insult' which is 'stealing the soul of millions.'[10] It is clear that the recent acts of destruction were not arbitrary or illogical acts, but rather constituted a multifaceted tactic to disrupt society as part of a premeditated and sophisticated strategy to expand the Islamic empire.[11]

The recent destruction of cultural heritage has been universally condemned.[12] For example, the African Commission on Human and Peoples' Rights declared that the 'barbaric and unspeakable acts' of

> destruction and desecration of the mausoleums of Muslim saints and other ancient sites of the mythical city of Timbuktu ... are inconsistent with the African Charter on Human and Peoples' Rights and other African and international legal instruments on human rights and international humanitarian law.[13]

---

9 The report also states that '[a]ffected people are suffering from the disruption of their cultural practices, skills and expressions of intangible cultural heritage. In the longer-term, if these populations are left without a prospect for the safe return to their homes the cultural diversity in Iraq and Syria will be irreversibly lost.' UNESCO, 'Background Note to the International Conference "Heritage and Cultural Diversity at Risk in Iraq and Syria" – The Protection of Heritage and Cultural Diversity: A Humanitarian and Security Imperative in the Conflicts of the 21st Century', UNESCO Headquarters, Paris (3 December 2014), 7.
10 John Kerry, *Remarks at Threats to Cultural Heritage in Iraq and Syria* (22 September 2014) http://www.state.gov/secretary/remarks/2014/09/231992htm accessed 10 November 2019.
11 Paolo Foradori and Paolo Rosa, 'Expanding the Peacekeeping Agenda. The Protection of Cultural Heritage in War-Torn Societies' (2017) 29(2) *Global Change, Peace and Security* 145, 148.
12 See, for example, European Parliament, Resolution on Syria of 19 June 2015 and Resolution on the destruction of cultural sites perpetrated by ISIS/Da'esh (30 April 2015); African Commission on Human and Peoples' Rights, 'Press Release on the Destruction of Cultural and Ancient Monuments in the Malian City of Timbuktu' (10 July 2012) http://www.achpr.org/pressrelease/detail?id=292 accessed 20 February 2020; African Union, 'Solemn Declaration on Situation in Mali' (19 July 2012) https://reliefweb.int/report/mali/solemn-declaration-assembly-union-situation-mali accessed 19 February 2020.
13 African Commission on Human and Peoples' Rights, 'Press Release on the Destruction of Cultural and Ancient Monuments in the Malian City of Timbuktu' (10 July 2012) http://www.achpr.org/press/2012/07/d115/ accessed 10 November 2019.

4 Introduction

Despite the global condemnation of attacks on cultural heritage,

> concrete action to halt the crime in question has been quite limited so far, in terms not only of *ex-post* reactions against the worst cases of destruction of cultural heritage, but also of prevention of such destruction when it is likely to happen.[14]

While a legal framework exists, which seeks to protect cultural heritage, including the 1954 Hague Convention for the Protection of Cultural Property in the Event of Armed Conflict,[15] legal instruments were seen as ineffective in the face of the recent attacks. Foradori and Rosa thus comment that '[t]he unprecedented levels of systematic destruction of cultural heritage by ISIS ... has sparked international outrage and triggered an urgent reflection on how to ensure the enforcement of the 1954 Convention.'[16] While the International Criminal Court (ICC) has recently addressed the question of individual criminal responsibility in respect of attacks on cultural sites in Mali in the case of *Prosecutor v Al Mahdi*,[17] this is, obviously, case-specific and therefore an inadequate response to the general destruction of cultural heritage.

The focus on cultural heritage as a target of conflict, rather than collateral damage, requires us to reassess the extant legal framework which seeks to protect cultural heritage during armed conflict. While a complex legal web of instruments exists which aim to protect cultural heritage during armed conflict, these instruments have failed to facilitate an effective response by the international community to the increasing threats to cultural heritage we have recently witnessed. Despite the universal condemnation of attacks on cultural heritage, an effective international response has remained elusive.[18] In this context, Luck comments that

> [t]he threat to cultural heritage is emerging as a first-tier challenge to the established international order, yet it has been treated until now as a

---

14 Federico Lenzerini, 'Terrorism, Conflicts and the Responsibility to Protect Cultural Heritage' (2016) 51(2) *The International Spectator* 70, 79.
15 Convention for the Protection of Cultural Property in the Event of Armed Conflict, adopted at The Hague, 1954, 249 UNTS 240.
16 Paolo Foradori and Paolo Rosa, 'Expanding the Peacekeeping Agenda. The protection of Cultural Heritage in War-Torn Societies' (2017) 29(2) *Global Change, Peace and Security* 145, 150.
17 *Prosecutor v Al Mahdi* ICC-01/12-01/15. A second case concerning attacks on cultural heritage sites in Mali is currently before the ICC. See *Prosecutor v Al Hassan Ag Abdoul Aziz Ag Mohamed Ag Mahmoud* ICC-01/12-01/18.
18 Edward C Luck, 'Cultural Genocide and the Protection of Cultural Heritage', J Paul Getty Trust Occasional Papers in Cultural Heritage Policy, Number 2 (2018), 6.

Introduction 5

second- or third-tier policy priority. Unless this gap is narrowed, efforts to protect cultural heritage against these growing threats will fall tragically short.[19]

Petrovic comments that 'the changing nature of armed conflict has brought onto the battleground new actors who increasingly misuse cultural property to advance their agenda. The cultural warfare requires that the international community's responses follow the changes on the ground.'[20] The international community has responded by suggesting new paradigms for the protection of cultural heritage, and this book assesses the effectiveness of these paradigms. Previously, various paradigms for the protection of cultural heritage were identified; for example, Frulli divides the original international law response to protecting cultural heritage during conflict into two, i.e. the 'civilian use' paradigm and the 'culture-value' paradigm.[21] In response to recent attacks on cultural heritage, however, international organisations and academics have suggested new approaches to the protection of cultural heritage during armed conflict. Bokova's labelling of attacks on cultural heritage in Iraq and Syria as 'cultural cleansing' has ignited a discussion on the utility of applying a Responsibility to Protect framework to the protection of cultural property, for example,[22] and there has also been some urging in academia to return to a cultural genocide paradigm to address this issue.[23]

---

19 Ibid., 5. Luck also comments (at 6) that '[i]t has been difficult for states to agree on or to mount an effective, coherent, and sustained protection campaign. Though media coverage and the courageous testimonies of those who have sought to preserve this heritage have brought wide attention to the issue, the international community still has not converged on a legal, political, or institutional framework for pursuing effective protection efforts. Policy actions have been sporadic, even hesitant. As in other areas of public policy, practical or operational shortfalls often stem from the lack of convergence on larger principles, concepts, and strategy – all things that flow from a shared framing or understanding of the challenges at hand.'
20 Jadranka Petrovic, 'The Cultural Dimension of Peace Operations: Peacekeeping and Cultural Property', in Andrew H Campbell (ed), *Global Leadership Initiatives for Conflict Resolution and Peacebuilding* (IGI Global, 2018), 84, 102.
21 Michaela Frulli, 'The Criminalization of Offences against Cultural Heritage in Times of Armed Conflict: The Quest for Consistency' (2011) 22(1) *European Journal of International Law* 203.
22 See, for example, James Cuno, 'The Responsibility to Protect the World's Cultural Heritage' (2016) 23 Brown J World Affairs 97; Federico Lenzerini, 'Terrorism, Conflicts and the Responsibility to Protect Cultural Heritage' (2016) 51(2) *The International Spectator* 70; and Hugh Eakin, 'Use Force to Stop ISIS' Destruction of Art and History', *New York Times* (3 April 2015).
23 See, for example, Edward C Luck, 'Cultural Genocide and the Protection of Cultural Heritage', J Paul Getty Trust Occasional Papers in Cultural Heritage Policy, Number 2 (2018).

6 *Introduction*

Significantly, the UN has now placed the protection of cultural heritage during armed conflict within a security paradigm,[24] and the Security Council has adopted a number of resolutions on the topic, highlighting the protection of cultural heritage as an international peace and security issue.[25] This has led to the emergence of cultural peacekeeping and an emphasis on cultural heritage in peacebuilding initiatives.[26]

What is cultural heritage?

This book focuses on the protection of cultural heritage during armed conflict. The terms *cultural property* and *cultural heritage* are both used in legal instruments and in academic commentary,[27] although the term *heritage* is recognised as being broader than *property* and is the preferred term in this book.[28]

There is no universally accepted definition of these concepts, but various international legal instruments set out a definition of cultural property/heritage for the purposes of that specific legal instrument. According to Petrovic,

> [d]espite the varied definitions across the international instruments there is an agreement that cultural property is a unique property which underpins human wellbeing and flourishing. … [it] forms a vital part of the cultural identity of individuals, groups, communities and peoples

---

24 See Paolo Foradori and Paolo Rosa, 'Expanding the Peacekeeping Agenda. The Protection of Cultural Heritage in War-Torn Societies' (2017) 29(2) *Global Change, Peace & Security* 145.
25 UN SC Resolution 2347 (2017).
26 See Paolo Foradori and Paolo Rosa, 'Expanding the Peacekeeping Agenda. The Protection of Cultural Heritage in War-Torn Societies' (2017) 29(2) *Global Change, Peace & Security* 145. In relation to cultural aspects of peacekeeping, see Tamara Duffey, 'Cultural Issues In Contemporary Peacekeeping' (2000) 7(1) *International Peacekeeping* 141.
27 See Manlio Frigo, 'Cultural property v. Cultural Heritage: A "Battle of Concepts" in International Law?' (2004) 86(854) *International Review of the Red Cross* 367; Lyndel V Prott and Patrick J O'Keefe, '"Cultural Heritage" or 'Cultural Property'?' (1992) 1 *International Journal of Cultural Property* 307.
28 Writing in 1992, Prott and O'Keefe asked: 'Is it time for law and lawyers to recognize that the term "cultural heritage" is rightfully superseding that of "cultural property"?' They answered in the affirmative, because, first, 'the existing legal concept of "property" does not, and should not try to, cover all that evidence of human life that we are trying to preserve: those things and traditions which express the way of life and thought of a particular society; which are evidence of its intellectual and spiritual achievements', and second, '"property" does not incorporate concepts of duty to preserve and protect.' Ibid., 307.

... [and] also constitutes an irreplaceable part of humanity's shared cultural heritage.[29]

Research question

Given the significant and, potentially, irreparable, damage which has been caused to cultural heritage in recent times, it is essential that the international community reacts with an effective multidimensional response. This book seeks to assess the traditional legal framework applicable to the protection of cultural heritage during armed conflict and then to evaluate various paradigms which have been recently proposed to increase this protection.

Structure

In order to adequately address the research question, the first chapter of the book traces the development of the legal framework on the protection of cultural heritage during armed conflict. The second chapter discusses three interrelated paradigms which could enhance the protection of cultural heritage and questions their effectiveness: cultural cleansing, the Responsibility to Protect doctrine, and cultural genocide. The final chapter examines recent initiatives by international organisations to apply a security paradigm to the destruction of cultural heritage.

---

29 Jadranka Petrovic, 'The Cultural Dimension of Peace Operations: Peacekeeping and Cultural Property', in Andrew H Campbell (ed), *Global Leadership Initiatives for Conflict Resolution and Peacebuilding* (IGI Global, 2018), 84, 87.

1 Traditional paradigms on the protection of cultural heritage during armed conflict

Introduction

The deliberate destruction of cultural heritage has been a continuing, and frequently occurring, phenomenon throughout history,[1] and has been well documented.[2] An early recorded example of such destruction is the demolition of the Temple of Serapis in Alexandria, Egypt, in 391 AD, on the orders of Roman Emperor Theodosius, with the aim of destroying the last sanctuary of non-Christians.[3] More recent examples include the razing of synagogues and other Jewish cultural sites in the Old City of Jerusalem after its subjugation by the Arab Legion in 1948;[4] the demolition of mosques and other religious or historic buildings during the Balkan Wars in the 1990s;[5]

---

1 Francesco Francioni and Federico Lenzerini, 'The Destruction of the Buddhas of Bamiyan and International Law' (2003) 14(4) *European Journal of International Law* 619, 619.
2 See Jiri Toman, *The Protection of Cultural Property in the Event of Armed Conflict* (Dartmouth Publishing Company 1996); Roger O'Keefe, *The Protection of Cultural Property during Armed Conflict* (Cambridge University Press 2006); Ana Filipa Vrdoljak, 'The Criminalisation of the Intentional Destruction of Cultural Heritage' in Tiffany Bergin and Emanuela Orlando (eds), *Forging a Socio-Legal Approach to Environmental Harms. Global Perspectives* (Routledge 2017), 237.
3 Francesco Francioni and Federico Lenzerini, 'The Destruction of the Buddhas of Bamiyan and International Law' (2003) 14(4) *European Journal of International Law* 619, 620.
4 Federico Lenzerini, 'Terrorism, Conflicts and the Responsibility to Protect Cultural Heritage' (2016) 51(2) *The International Spectator* 70, 71.
5 See Helen Walasek et al., *Bosnia and the Destruction of Cultural Heritage* (Routledge 2016). See also Hirad Abtathi, 'The Protection of Cultural Property in Times of Armed Conflict: The Practice of the International Criminal Tribunal for the Former Yugoslavia' (2001) 14 *Harvard Human Rights Journal* 1; Theodor Meron, 'The Protection of Cultural Property in the Event of Armed Conflict within the Case-law of the International Criminal Tribunal for the Former Yugoslavia' (2005) 57(4) *Museum International* 41; Marc Balcells, 'Left Behind? Cultural Destruction, the Role of the International Criminal Tribunal for the Former Yugoslavia in Deterring it and Cultural Heritage Prevention Policies in the Aftermath of the Balkan Wars' (2015) 21(1) *European Journal on Criminal Policy and Research* 1.

the attacks on the two ancient Bamiyan Buddha statues in Afghanistan by the Taliban in 2001, which was part of a wider plan to eradicate all elements of non-Muslim cultures in the area;[6] and the recent destruction of multiple cultural sites in Timbuktu, Mali, by the extremist group Ansar Dine in June–July 2012.[7] As highlighted by Lenzerini,

> [i]n all these cases, the perpetrators' actions were driven by a persecutory intent. In some of the examples, the targeted community was all of humanity not belonging to the perpetrators' groups, as their iconoclasm was based on the fantastic delirium that truth lies only in what is representative of one's own culture, while manifestations of different cultures are to be obliterated forever.[8]

Attacks on cultural heritage were first prohibited in the period between the close of the 19th century and the start of the 20th century. However, 'the protection devoted to such property at that time remained at an embryonic level.'[9] It is interesting to note that the concept of 'culture' was not a part of the legal vernacular at this time, with the first legal instruments prohibiting attacks on cultural heritage not even using the term *culture*. Rather, the Hague Conventions on the Laws and Customs of War of 1899 and 1907 state that '[i]n sieges and bombardments all necessary steps should be taken to spare as far as possible edifices devoted to religion, art, science, and charity [...] provided they are not used at the same time for military purposes.'[10] Lenzerini comments that at this point in time, 'the rationale of the protection of the property concerned was merely a corollary of state sovereignty,

---

6 Francesco Francioni and Federico Lenzerini, 'The Destruction of the Buddhas of Bamiyan and International Law' (2003) 14(4) *European Journal of International Law* 619, 619; Bren Whitney Bren, 'Terrorists and Antiquities: Lessons from the Destruction of the Bamiyan Buddhas, Current ISIS Aggression, and a Proposed Framework for Cultural Property Crimes' (2016) 34(1) *Cardozo Arts & Entertainment Law Journal* 215.
7 See Mohamed Elewa Badar and Noelle Higgins, 'Discussion Interrupted: The Destruction and Protection of Cultural Property under International Law and Islamic Law – the Case of *Prosecutor v. Al Mahdi*' (2017) 17(3) *International Criminal Law Review* 486; Mohamed Elewa Badar and Noelle Higgins, 'The Destruction of Cultural Property in Timbuktu: Challenging the ICC War Crime Paradigm' (2017) 74(3/4) *Europa Ethnica* 99.
8 Federico Lenzerini, 'Terrorism, Conflicts and the Responsibility to Protect Cultural Heritage' (2016) 51(2) *The International Spectator* 70, 72.
9 Ibid.
10 Article 27 of Hague Convention II with Respect to the Laws and Customs of War on Land and its annex: Regulation concerning the Laws and Customs of War on Land, 1899; Article 27 of the Regulations annexed to Hague Convention IV with Respect to the Laws and Customs of War on Land, 1907; and Article 5 of Hague Convention IX concerning Bombardment by Naval Forces in Time of War, 1907.

while no value was attributed to it as a heritage belonging to humanity as a whole.'[11] Over time, however, the rationale for the protection of cultural heritage has changed as its role as identity marker, and its value to the local, and indeed, global, community has become recognised. This change in rationale is reflected in the wording of the legal instruments adopted with the aim of its protection.

This chapter analyses the traditional paradigms on the protection of cultural heritage during armed conflict and their development over time. The first section sets out the legal framework concerning the prohibition of attacks on cultural heritage, highlighting the rationales for such protection. The second section focuses on individual criminal responsibility for crimes against culture and analyses the international jurisprudence on this issue prior to the adoption of the Rome Statute of the International Criminal Court (ICC). The third section then discusses the approach the ICC takes to attacks on cultural heritage.

The legal framework protecting cultural heritage

History books abound with examples of the condemnation of the destruction of cultural heritage during times of armed conflict. For example, in the 2nd century BC, Polybius, a Greek historian, criticised the plundering of art by the Romans after their defeat of Syracuse in 212 BC.[12] Later, in 146 BC, Cicero reports that after the siege and capture of Carthage, Scipio Aemilianus, commander of the final siege, arranged to have various works of art that Carthage had stolen from the Greek cities of Sicily returned to their owners, rather than keeping them for himself.[13] Later, international legal scholars addressed the issue of the destruction of cultural heritage. For example, in 1625 Grotius discussed the question of whether pillaging during armed conflict could be justified, and referred back to the opinions of Polybius and Cicero.[14] He stated that '[t]here are some things of such a

---

11 Federico Lenzerini, 'Terrorism, Conflicts and the Responsibility to Protect Cultural Heritage' (2016) 51(2) *The International Spectator* 70, 73.
12 Polybius, trans by Robin Waterfield, *Book IX: The Histories* (Oxford University Press 2010). See also US Committee of the Blue Shield, 'History of Protection of Cultural Property: Ancient Authors' https://uscbs.org/antiquity.html accessed 10 November 2019.
13 See US Committee of the Blue Shield, 'History of Protection of Cultural Property: Ancient Authors' https://uscbs.org/antiquity.html accessed 10 November 2019. See also M Tullius Cicero, trans by CD Yonge, *The Orations of Marcus Tullius Cicero* (George Bel & Sons 1903).
14 Hugo Grotius, trans by AC Campbell, *The Rights of War and Peace, including the Law of Nature and of Nations* (M Walter Dunne 1901), Book III, Chapter XII.

nature, as to contribute, no way, to the support and prolongation of war: things which reason itself requires to be spared even during the heat and continuance of war.'[15] De Vattel, in 1758, called for a prohibition of the plundering of works of art and architecture in his work *The Law of Nations*, stating:

> For whatever reason a belligerent plunders a country, he should spare buildings that are the pride of mankind and do not strengthen the enemy. Temples, tombstones, public buildings, and all other works of art distinguished for their beauty; what can be the advantage of destroying them? Only an enemy of mankind can thoughtlessly deprive humanity of those monuments of art, the exemplars of artistry.[16]

While condemnation of attacks on cultural heritage during armed conflict have been noted throughout history, the prohibition on such attacks came much later. Indeed, it was not until the 19th century that such attacks were legally forbidden. The legal framework has expanded and developed significantly since this time, and it now consists of a complex web of instruments and jurisprudence.[17] Numerous legal sources seek to proscribe attacks on cultural heritage, and the international legal framework reflects several divergent paradigms on, and rationales for, its protection. Some international instruments seek to prohibit attacks on cultural property because such property constitutes civilian, rather than military, property, while others underline the need to protect cultural heritage because of its importance to humanity, and others again focus on prohibiting the illicit trade in cultural goods and link such trade with the fuelling of conflict.

Early international law instruments seeking to protect cultural heritage include 19th-century documents such as the Lieber Code 1863,[18] the 1874 Declaration of Brussels,[19] the 1880 Oxford Manual,[20] and the Hague

---

15 Ibid., Chapter XII.V.
16 Emer de Vattel, edited and with Introduction by Béla Kapossy and Richard Whitmore, *The Law of Nations or the Principles of Natural Law Applied to the Conduct and to the Affairs of Nations and of Sovereigns* (Liberty Fund 2008), Book III, Chapter IX, §168.
17 Marina Lostal, *International Cultural Heritage Law in Armed Conflict* (Cambridge University Press 2017), 3.
18 Instructions for the Government of Armies of the United States in the Field. Prepared by Francis Lieber, promulgated as General Orders No. 100 by President Lincoln, 24 April 1863.
19 Project of an International Declaration concerning the Laws and Customs of War, signed at Brussels, 27 August 1874.
20 The Laws of War on Land, Manual published by the Institute of International Law (Oxford Manual), adopted by the Institute of International Law at Oxford, 9 September 1880.

12 *Traditional paradigms*

Regulations 1899.[21] 34 of the Lieber Code, an instrument which was commissioned by President Abraham Lincoln during the American Civil War for use by Union soldiers, states:

> As a general rule, the property belonging to churches, to hospitals, or other establishments of an exclusively charitable character, to establishments of education, or foundations for the promotion of knowledge, whether public schools, universities, academies of learning or observatories, museums of the fine arts, or of a scientific character such property is not to be considered public property in the sense of paragraph 31; but it may be taxed or used when the public service may require it.[22]

Article 35 provides that 'classical works of art, libraries, scientific collections, or precious instruments ... must be secured against all avoidable injury.'[23]

The Brussels Declaration of 1874, in addition to the Hague Regulations on the Laws and Customs of War on Land of 1899 and 1907, is partly based on the Lieber Code, and all of these instruments echo the principle that cultural heritage should be protected in times of armed conflict. The Brussels Declaration was drafted on the initiative of Czar Alexander II of Russia, whose government submitted the draft of an international agreement on the laws and customs of war to a meeting of delegates from 15 European States in Brussels on 27 July 1874. While the Conference adopted the draft with minor alterations, some governments were reluctant to accept it as a binding convention, and it was, therefore, not ratified. However, the project marked an important step in the development of the codification of the laws of war. Article 8 of this instrument states that

---

Article 53 states that 'The property of municipalities, and that of institutions devoted to religion, charity, education, art and science, cannot be seized. All destruction or wilful damage to institutions of this character, historic monuments, archives, Works of art, or science, is formally forbidden, save when urgently demanded by military necessity.'

21 Hague Convention II with Respect to the Laws and Customs of War on Land and its annex: Regulations concerning the Laws and Customs of War on Land, 29 July 1899. Annex to the Convention; Regulations respecting the Laws and Customs of War on Land.

22 Article 34, Instructions for the Government of Armies of the United States in the Field. Prepared by Francis Lieber, promulgated as General Orders No. 100 by President Lincoln, 24 April 1863.

23 Article 35, Instructions for the Government of Armies of the United States in the Field. Prepared by Francis Lieber, promulgated as General Orders No. 100 by President Lincoln, 24 April 1863.

[t]he property of municipalities, that of institutions dedicated to religion, charity and education, the arts and sciences even when State property, shall be treated as private property. All seizure or destruction of, or wilful damage to, institutions of this character, historic monuments, works of art and science should be made the subject of legal proceedings by the competent authorities.[24]

Article 17 provides that

[i]n such cases [of bombardment of a defended town or fortress, agglomeration of dwellings, or village] all necessary steps must be taken to spare, as far as possible, buildings dedicated to art, science, or charitable purposes, hospitals ... provided they are not being used at the time for military purposes. It is the duty of the besieged to indicate the presence of such buildings by distinctive and visible signs to be communicated to the enemy beforehand.[25]

In 1874, the Institute of International Law appointed a committee to review the Brussels Declaration and to submit additional proposals on its subject matter. The work of the Institute led to the adoption of the Manual of the Laws and Customs of War at Oxford in 1880,[26] Article 34 of which states that

[i]n case of bombardment all necessary steps must be taken to spare, if it can be done, buildings dedicated to religion, art, science and charitable purposes ... on the condition that they are not being utilized at the time, directly or indirectly, for defense. It is the duty of the besieged to indicate the presence of such buildings by visible signs notified to the assailant beforehand.[27]

---

24 Article 8, Project of an International Declaration concerning the Laws and Customs of War, signed at Brussels, 27 August 1874.
25 Article 17, Project of an International Declaration concerning the Laws and Customs of War, signed at Brussels, 27 August 1874.
26 The Laws of War on Land, Manual published by the Institute of International Law (Oxford Manual), adopted by the Institute of International Law at Oxford, September 9, 1880. Article 53 states that 'The property of municipalities, and that of institutions devoted to religion, charity, education, art and science, cannot be seized. All destruction or wilful damage to institutions of this character, historic monuments, archives, works of art, or science, is formally forbidden, save when urgently demanded by military necessity.'
27 Article 34, The Laws of War on Land, Manual published by the Institute of International Law (Oxford Manual), adopted by the Institute of International Law at Oxford, 1880.

14 Traditional paradigms

Both the Brussels Declaration and the Oxford Manual provided a framework for the Hague Conventions on land warfare and the Regulations annexed to them, adopted in 1899 and 1907. The first Hague Peace Conference was convened in 1899, with the aim of revising the declaration that had been set forth, but never ratified, by the Conference of Brussels in 1874 concerning the laws and customs of war. The resulting instrument, the 1899 Hague Convention on land warfare, was adopted and subsequently ratified by 50 States Parties. The 1899 Convention was revised at the Second International Peace Conference in October 1907, and it is now accepted that these provisions reflect customary law.

Article 23(g) of the 1899 Convention states that it is forbidden 'to destroy or seize the enemy's property, unless such destruction or seizure be imperatively demanded by the necessities of war.'[28] Article 25 further states that 'the attack or bombardment of towns, villages, habitations or buildings which are not defended, is prohibited.'[29] Article 27 also provides that

> in sieges and bombardments all necessary steps should be taken to spare as far as possible edifices devoted to religion, art, science, and charity, hospitals, and places where the sick and wounded are collected, provided they are not used at the same time for military purposes.

Moreover, 'the besieged should indicate these buildings or places by some particular and visible signs, which should previously be notified to the assailants.'[30] Article 28 then provides that '[t]he pillage of a town or place, even when taken by assault is prohibited.'[31] Finally, Article 56 states that

> the property of municipalities, that of institutions dedicated to religion, charity and education, the arts and sciences, even when State property, shall be treated as private property. All seizure of, destruction or wilful damage done to institutions of this character, historic monuments,

---

28 Article 23(g), Convention II with Respect to the Laws and Customs of War on Land and its annex: Regulations concerning the Laws and Customs of War on Land, 29 July 1899.
29 Article 25, Convention II with Respect to the Laws and Customs of War on Land and its annex: Regulations concerning the Laws and Customs of War on Land, 29 July 1899.
30 Articles 27, Convention II with Respect to the Laws and Customs of War on Land and its annex: Regulations concerning the Laws and Customs of War on Land, 1899. Annex to the Convention; Regulations respecting the Laws and Customs of War on Land.
31 Article 28, Convention II with Respect to the Laws and Customs of War on Land and its annex: Regulations concerning the Laws and Customs of War on Land, 1899. Annex to the Convention; Regulations respecting the Laws and Customs of War on Land.

works of art and science, is forbidden, and should be made the subject of legal proceedings.[32]

Nearly identical provisions are included in the 1907 Convention, with only a few minor changes in wording. Furthermore, the 1919 Commission on Responsibility of the Authors of the War and on Enforcement of Penalties, a commission established at the Paris Peace Conference with the role of examining the context of World War I and recommending individuals for prosecution for committing war crimes, identified 'wanton destruction of religious, charitable, educational, and historic buildings and monuments' as a war crime.[33]

While early writings on the subject decried attacks on cultural heritage because of its value to humanity, as already highlighted, the legal framework took a different stance. One of the basic principles of international humanitarian law is the principle of distinction, which requires that civilian objects not be the object of attack,[34] and this is the underpinning rationale and paradigm for the prohibition of the destruction of cultural heritage in the instruments discussed above. In these instruments, the protection of cultural property is paralleled with the protection of other civilian objects, including hospitals and religious sites, and its importance to humanity is not acknowledged as a reason for its protection.

However, later international legal instruments recognised the need to protect cultural property because of its value to humanity.[35] Three conventions in particular – the 1954 Hague Convention for the Protection of Cultural

---

32 Article 56, Convention II with Respect to the Laws and Customs of War on Land and its annex: Regulations concerning the Laws and Customs of War on Land. The Hague, 29 July 1899. Annex to the Convention; Regulations respecting the Laws and Customs of War on Land.
33 Commission on the Responsibility of the Authors of the War and on Enforcement of Penalties, 'Report Presented to the Preliminary Peace Conference' (1920) 14 *American Journal of International Law* 95, 115.
34 International Committee of the Red Cross Customary IHL Rule 7 states that 'The parties to the conflict must at all times distinguish between civilian objects and military objectives. Attacks may only be directed against military objectives. Attacks must not be directed against civilian objects.' Jean-Marie Henckaerts and Louise Doswald-Beck (eds), *Customary Humanitarian Law. Volume I: Rules* (ICRC/Cambridge University Press 2005). See Customary IHL Database www.icrc.org/en/war-and-law/treaties-customary-law/cust omary-law accessed 10 November 2019.
35 While the Roerich Pact does not set out a rationale for the protection of cultural property, the previous work of the initiator, Nicholas Roerich, in bringing states together to protect such property illustrates his belief that 'the cultural heritage of each nation is in essence a world treasure.' See Nicholas Roerich Museum website, www.roerich.org/roerich-pact. php accessed 2 October 2017. The Roerich Pact was signed in the White House, in the

16 Traditional paradigms

Property in the Event of Armed Conflict and its two (1954 and 1999) Protocols,[36] the 1970 United Nations Educational, Scientific and Cultural Organization (UNESCO) Convention on the Means of Prohibiting and Preventing the Illicit Import, Export and Transfer of Ownership of Cultural Property,[37] and the 1972 UNESCO Convention Concerning the Protection of the World Cultural and Natural Heritage[38] – reflect the view that attacks on cultural heritage are attacks on the shared identity of humankind.[39]

The first of these instruments, i.e. the Hague Convention for the Protection of Cultural Property in the Event of Armed Conflict, adopted in 1954, provides in its preamble that 'damage to cultural property belonging to any people whatsoever means damage to the cultural heritage of all mankind.'[40] Thus, we see a recognition of the opinions of the early writers on this subject, such as Cicero and de Vattel, that cultural heritage should be protected during armed conflict, not merely because its destruction can provide no military advantage, but also because of its inherent value to humanity. The 1954 Convention was the first international treaty dedicated solely to the issue of protection of cultural heritage, and 'marked the beginning of an era in international law in which cultural items became objects worthy of independent legal concern in their own right.'[41] This Convention

---

presence of President Franklin Delano Roosevelt, on 15 April 1935, by all the members of the PanAmerican Union, and later, by other States.
36 Convention for the Protection of Cultural Property in the Event of Armed Conflict, adopted at The Hague, 1954, 249 UNTS 240. First Protocol to the Convention for the Protection of Cultural Property in the Event of Armed Conflict 1954, adopted at The Hague, 14 May 1954, 249 UNTS 358. Second Protocol to the Convention for the Protection of Cultural Property in the Event of Armed Conflict 1954, adopted at The Hague, 26 March 1999, 2252 UNTS 172.
37 UNESCO Convention on the Means of Prohibiting and Preventing the Illicit Import, Export and Transfer of Ownership of Cultural Property, adopted at Paris, 14 November 1970, 823 UNTS 231.
38 World Heritage Convention Concerning the Protection of the World Cultural and Natural Heritage, adopted at Paris, 16 November 1972.
39 UNESCO, *Report of the International Conference 'Heritage and Cultural Diversity at Risk in Iraq and Syria'* (2014), 24 www.unesco.org/culture/pdf/iraq-syria/IraqSyriaReport-en.pdf accessed 10 November 2019.
40 Preamble, Convention for the Protection of Cultural Property in the Event of Armed Conflict, adopted at The Hague, 1954, 249 UNTS 240. Article 1 of this instrument defines cultural property as 'any movable or immovable property of great importance to the cultural heritage of all people, such as monuments of architecture or history, archaeological sites, works of art, books or any building whose main and effective purpose is to contain cultural property.'
41 Marina Lostal, *International Cultural Heritage Law in Armed Conflict* (Cambridge University Press 2017), 62.

is supplemented by two protocols;[42] the First Protocol[43] focuses on the restitution of cultural property unlawfully removed in connection with an armed conflict, while the Second Protocol[44] established a new category of enhanced protection for cultural heritage that is particularly important for humankind. These instruments are complemented by the 1949 Geneva Conventions and the 1977 Protocols.[45]

The UNESCO Convention on the Means of Prohibiting and Preventing the Illicit Import, Export and Transfer of Ownership of Cultural Property[46] was adopted in 1970. Its primary focus is not on the protection of cultural heritage during armed conflict, but rather on combatting the illegal trade in cultural items. It is a 'cornerstone of cultural heritage law, creating multilateral control over the movement of cultural property while seeking to promote its legitimate exchange and international cooperation in preparing national inventories of it.'[47] The preamble of this instrument states that 'the interchange of cultural property among nations for scientific, cultural and educational purposes increases the knowledge of the civilization of Man, enriches the cultural life of all peoples and inspires mutual respect and appreciation among nations.'[48] While the Convention does not specifically

---

42 First Protocol to the Convention for the Protection of Cultural Property in the Event of Armed Conflict 1954, adopted at The Hague, 14 May 1954, 249 UNTS 358; and Second Protocol to the Convention for the Protection of Cultural Property in the Event of Armed Conflict 1954, adopted at The Hague, 26 March 1999, 2252 UNTS 172.
43 First Protocol to the Convention for the Protection of Cultural Property in the Event of Armed Conflict 1954, adopted at The Hague, 14 May 1954, 249 UNTS 358.
44 Second Protocol to the Convention for the Protection of Cultural Property in the Event of Armed Conflict 1954, adopted at The Hague, 26 March 1999, 2252 UNTS 172.
45 Geneva Convention for the Amelioration of the Condition of the Wounded and Sick in Armed Forces in the Field (First Geneva Convention), Geneva Convention for the Amelioration of the Condition of Wounded, Sick and Shipwrecked Members of Armed Forces at Sea (Second Geneva Convention), Geneva Convention relative to the Treatment of Prisoners of War (Third Geneva Convention), and Geneva Convention Relative to the Protection of Civilian Persons in Time of War (Fourth Geneva Convention), adopted 12 August 1949; Protocol Additional to the Geneva Conventions of 12 August 1949, and relating to the Protection of Victims of International Armed Conflicts (Protocol I), 8 June 1977 and Protocol Additional to the Geneva Conventions of 12 August 1949, and relating to the Protection of Victims of Non-International Armed Conflicts (Protocol II), 8 June 1977.
46 UNESCO Convention on the Means of Prohibiting and Preventing the Illicit Import, Export and Transfer of Ownership of Cultural Property, adopted at Paris, 14 November 1970, 823 UNTS 231.
47 James AR Nafziger, Robert Kirkwood Paterson, and Alison Dundes Renteln (eds), *Cultural Law* (Cambridge University Press 2010), 289.
48 Preamble, UNESCO Convention on the Means of Prohibiting and Preventing the Illicit Import, Export and Transfer of Ownership of Cultural Property, adopted at Paris, 14 November 1970, 823 UNTS 231.

deal with the destruction of cultural heritage during armed conflict, it does include reference to the reasons why a legal framework is necessary for its protection, stating in its preamble that 'cultural property constitutes one of the basic elements of civilization and national culture.'[49] The focus of this instrument is also the subject of the UNIDROIT Convention on Stolen or Illegally Exported Cultural Objects, adopted in 1995, which, in its preamble, highlights 'the fundamental importance of the protection of cultural heritage and of cultural exchanges for promoting understanding between peoples, and the dissemination of culture for the well-being of humanity and the progress of civilisation.'[50]

The 1972 World Heritage Convention Concerning the Protection of the World Cultural and Natural Heritage applies during armed conflict as well as during peacetime.[51] Under Article 6(3), States Parties are obliged to refrain from taking any deliberate measures which may damage, directly or indirectly, the world cultural heritage located on the territory of another state party. In addition, under Article 4, '[e]ach State Party … recognizes that the duty of ensuring the identification, protection, conservation, presentation and transmission to future generations of the cultural and natural heritage … situated on its territory, belongs primarily to that State.'[52]

The appreciation of the significance of cultural heritage and its role in enriching all of humanity was further developed at the start of the new century with the adoption of two Conventions by UNESCO – the Convention for the Safeguarding of the Intangible Cultural Heritage[53] in 2003 and the Convention on the Protection and Promotion of the Diversity of Cultural Expressions[54] in 2005 – both of which 'highlight the crucial importance that culture has for its creators and bearers, irrespective of its apparent value as perceived by "external" observers.'[55]

---

49 Ibid.
50 Preamble, UNIDROIT Convention on Stolen or Illegally Exported Cultural Objects, 24 June 1995, 34 ILM 1322.
51 World Heritage Convention Concerning the Protection of the World Cultural and Natural Heritage, adopted at Paris, 16 November 1972.
52 Article 4, World Heritage Convention Concerning the Protection of the World Cultural and Natural Heritage, adopted at Paris, 16 November 1972.
53 Convention for the Safeguarding of the Intangible Cultural Heritage, adopted at Paris, 17 October 2003.
54 Convention on the Protection and Promotion of the Diversity of Cultural Expressions, adopted at Paris, 20 October 2005.
55 Federico Lenzerini, 'Terrorism, Conflicts and the Responsibility to Protect Cultural Heritage' (2016) 51(2) *The International Spectator* 70, 71.

'Civilian use' and 'culture-value' paradigms on the protection of cultural heritage

Thus, reflecting on the instruments discussed above, we can appreciate two approaches to protecting cultural heritage in the international legal framework. These have been categorised by Frulli as the 'civilian use' paradigm and the 'culture-value' paradigm.[56] The former requires protection for cultural heritage as a result of its non-military nature, while the latter demands its protection because of its intrinsic value to humankind. Clear examples of the 'civilian use' approach can be identified in a number of the earlier instruments which include provisions on the protection of cultural heritage, including the Hague Conventions of 1899 and 1907, while the 'culture-value' approach can be appreciated in later instruments, including the 1954 Hague Convention and its Protocols, as well as the 1972 World Heritage Convention.

Lenzerini explains the importance of the culture-value paradigm on the protection of cultural heritage, stating that

> [a]wareness that cultural heritage plays a crucial role in the preservation of the cultural identity of peoples and communities – in some cases, as for most indigenous peoples, even of their very physical survival – paves the way for developing better legal protection not only for that heritage, but also for the human communities themselves.[57]

He emphasizes that '[t]he main – if not the only – reason for targeting cultural heritage as a hostile objective is the intent to persecute the communities for which that heritage represents an essential element of their cultural identity and distinctiveness.'[58] Thus, it is suggested, this rationale for the destruction of cultural heritage should be considered in the legal framework which seeks to protect it.

Human rights and cultural rights

The move to a broader understanding of cultural heritage – as property and artefacts having intrinsic value – was precipitated by growing attention

---

56 Michaela Frulli, 'The Criminalization of Offences against Cultural Heritage in Times of Armed Conflict: The Quest for Consistency' (2011) 22(1) *European Journal of International Law* 203.
57 Federico Lenzerini, 'Terrorism, Conflicts and the Responsibility to Protect Cultural Heritage' (2016) 51(2) *The International Spectator* 70, 71.
58 Ibid.

being placed on cultural rights and the rights of minorities at the United Nations (UN). Article 27 of the Universal Declaration of Human Rights, adopted in 1948, provides:

> (1) Everyone has the right freely to participate in the cultural life of the community, to enjoy the arts and to share in scientific advancement and its benefits.
> (2) Everyone has the right to the protection of the moral and material interests resulting from any scientific, literary or artistic production of which he is the author.[59]

The attainment of cultural rights has not progressed at the same pace as other categories of rights since 1948, and they have been described as the 'Cinderella' of human rights.[60] Work on the drafting of the International Covenant on Economic, Social and Cultural Rights began in 1948 and the instrument was adopted in 1966, thereby spanning the same period when the 1954 Convention on Cultural Property was being drafted. Thus, international attention was focused, to a certain extent, on the importance of culture during this time. Furthermore, the issue of minority rights, including their cultural rights, was also being discussed during this period at the UN, especially with regard to the crime of genocide and attacks on minority culture during World War II, which will be discussed in Chapter 2. While the concept of cultural genocide was not included within the definition of genocide adopted in the Genocide Convention 1948, the issue of minority rights and their cultural rights was included in the International Covenant on Civil and Political Rights, also adopted in 1966. Article 27 of this instrument states:

> In those States in which ethnic, religious or linguistic minorities exist, persons belonging to such minorities shall not be denied the right, in community with the other members of their group, to enjoy their own culture, to profess and practise their own religion, or to use their own language.[61]

The adoption of universal human rights treaties, which enshrined cultural rights and underscored the importance of culture, developed the international

---

59 Universal Declaration of Human Rights, proclaimed by the United Nations General Assembly in Paris on 10 December 1948 (General Assembly Resolution 217 A).
60 Minority Rights Group, 'Protecting the Right to Culture for Minorities and Indigenous Peoples: An Overview of International Case Law' *State of the World's Minorities and Indigenous Peoples 2016* (Minority Rights Group 2016), 61.
61 International Covenant on Civil and Political Rights, adopted by the General Assembly of the United Nations on 19 December 1966, 999 UNTS 171.

Traditional paradigms 21

discourse on, and understanding of, the concepts of culture and cultural heritage. This, in turn, impacted on the rationales for the protection of cultural heritage included in later international treaties. It is to be noted that the discourse on human rights has continued since this change in tone in respect of the protection of cultural heritage. In 2011, Farida Shaheed, the then UN Independent Expert in the Field of Cultural Rights, highlighted the interconnection between cultural heritage and human dignity and identity, and concluded that a right of access to, and enjoyment of, cultural heritage existed under international human rights law.[62] She stated that

> [t]o speak of cultural heritage in the context of human rights entails taking into consideration the multiple heritages through which individuals and communities express their humanity, give meaning to their existence, build their worldviews and represent their encounter with the external forces affecting their lives.[63]

Indeed, the UN has adopted a number of important documents in respect of cultural heritage and human rights, and has recognised the international destruction of cultural heritage as a violation of human rights.[64]

Customary international law

The divergent rationales identified by Frulli for the protection of cultural heritage have, to an extent, been merged in international customary law, with Customary Rule 38 of international humanitarian law stating that

A. Special care must be taken in military operations to avoid damage to buildings dedicated to religion, art, science, education or charitable purposes and historic monuments unless they are military objectives.
B. Property of great importance to the cultural heritage of every people must not be the object of attack unless imperatively required by military necessity.[65]

---

62 See Human Rights Council (17th Session) 'Report of Independent Expert in the Field of Cultural Rights, Farida Shaheed' (21 March 2011) A/HRC/17/38.
63 Ibid., para. 6.
64 See Office of the High Commissioner for Human Rights, 'The International Destruction of Cultural Heritage as a Violation of Human Rights', Report of the Special Rapporteur in the Field of Cultural Rights, Karima Bennoune (9 August 2016) UN Doc A/71/317.
65 Jean-Marie Henckaerts and Louise Doswald-Beck (eds), *Customary Humanitarian Law. Volume I: Rules* (ICRC/Cambridge University Press 2005).

22 Traditional paradigms

While customary international law recognises both the 'civilian use' and 'culture-value' rationales for the protection of cultural heritage, in practice a blurring of this binary framework has occurred.[66] A number of instruments, discussed above, provide for individual criminal responsibility over crimes relating to the destruction of cultural property, and the statutes of international criminal tribunals have also identified the destruction of cultural heritage as a war crime. In practice, these tribunals have recognised both a 'civilian use' approach and a 'culture-value' approach to the protection of cultural heritage and have developed this area of law, as will be discussed below.

Individual criminal responsibility for crimes against culture and the international criminal law jurisprudence

Individual criminal responsibility

Lostal comments that aim of the adoption of conventional laws for the protection of cultural property 'has mostly been motivated by a desire to hold individuals accountable,'[67] and a number of international conventions include provisions which allow for instituting criminal proceedings against individuals who commit violence against cultural heritage. For example, in times of occupation, the Hague Regulations stipulate that

> The property of municipalities, that of institutions dedicated to religion, charity and education, the arts, and sciences, even when State property, shall be treated as private property. All seizure of, destruction or wilful damage done to institutions of this character, historic monuments, works of art and science, is forbidden, and should be made the subject of legal proceedings.[68]

---

66 Article 4(f) of the Statute of the International Criminal Tribunal for Rwanda as established by Security Council Resolution 955 (1994) and Article 3(f) of the Statute of the Special Court for Sierra Leone as established pursuant to Security Council resolution 1315 (2000) mention only pillage as a war crime related to cultural property. Article 7 of the Law on the Establishment of the Extraordinary Chambers in the Courts of Cambodia for the Prosecution of Crimes Committed During the Period of Democratic Kampuchea (2001) (Cambodia) provides for prosecution pursuant to the provisions of the 1954 Hague Convention for the Protection of Cultural Property in the Event of Armed Conflict.
67 Marina Lostal, 'Syria's World Cultural Heritage and Individual Criminal Responsibility' (2015) 3 *International Review of Law* http://dx.doi.org/10.5339/irl.2015.3 accessed 1 November 2019.
68 Article 56, Convention IV respecting the Laws and Customs of War on Land and its annex: Regulations concerning the Laws and Customs of War on Land, adopted at The Hague, 18 October 1907.

It is reported[69] that Wilhelm Keitel and Alfred Rosenberg were prosecuted at the International Military Tribunal at Nuremberg[70] under the latter element of this provision for their role in the Reichsleiter Rosenberg Taskforce, which was dedicated to the appropriation of cultural heritage during World War II. Article 6(b) of the Charter of the International Military Tribunal at Nuremberg provided the Tribunal with jurisdiction over war crimes, including 'plunder of public or private property, wanton destruction of cities, towns or villages, or devastation not justified by military necessity.'[71] Both Keitel and Rosenberg were found guilty of plunder, amongst other crimes. This was the first time that prosecutions were instituted for theft of cultural property 'and demonstrate[d] an emergent will to award special treatment to cultural property *per se*.'[72]

According to Lostal, '[t]he wish to introduce mandatory punishment for individuals damaging, destroying or plundering cultural property was a key motivation behind the 1954 Hague Convention.'[73] Article 28 of this instrument provides that

> the High Contracting Parties undertake to take, within the framework of their ordinary criminal jurisdiction, all necessary steps to prosecute and impose penal or disciplinary sanctions upon those persons, of whatever nationality, who commit or order to be committed a breach of the present Convention.[74]

---

69 Suzanne L Schairer, 'The Intersection of Human Rights and Cultural Property Issues under International Law' (2001) 11 *Italian Yearbook of International Law* 59, 80.
70 See Article 6(b), Charter of the International Military Tribunal – Annex to the Agreement for the prosecution and punishment of the major war criminals of the European Axis ('London Agreement'), August 8, 1845, 82 UNTC, 280.
71 Agreement by the Government of the United Kingdom of Great Britain and Northern Ireland, the Government of the United States of America, the Provisional Government of the French Republic and the Government of the Union of Soviet Socialist Republics for the Prosecution and Punishment of the Major War Criminal of the European Axis, 82 UNTS 279, signed and entered into force 8 August 1945, annex. See also Article II(1)(b), Control Council Order No 10: Punishment of Persons Guilty of War Crimes, Crimes against Peace and against Humanity, 20 December 1945, (1946) 3 *Official Gazette Control Council for Germany* 50.
72 Marina Lostal, 'Syria's World Cultural Heritage and Individual Criminal Responsibility' (2015) 3 *International Review of Law* http://dx.doi.org/10.5339/irl.2015.3 accessed 10 November 2019.
73 Ibid., 10. See also Roger O'Keefe, 'Protection of Cultural Property under International Criminal Law' (2010) 11 *Melbourne Journal of International Law* 339, 359.
74 Article 28, Convention for the Protection of Cultural Property in the Event of Armed Conflict, adopted at The Hague, 1954, 249 UNTS 240.

24 Traditional paradigms

However, '[t]here is a generalised lack of implementation of the ... article into the domestic legal orders of state parties to the ... Convention.'[75]

Unfortunately, the 1972 World Heritage Convention omits a provision on individual criminal responsibility. However, significant momentum to criminalise crimes in respect of cultural heritage developed in the aftermath of the destruction of the Buddhas of Bamiyan in 2001. Lostal points out that the act was described as a 'crime against culture'[76] and also engendered the idea of 'crimes against the common heritage of humanity.'[77] The Declaration concerning the Intentional Destruction of Cultural Heritage was adopted in 2003 in response to the destruction of the Buddhas. This states that

> States should take all appropriate measures, in accordance with international law, to establish jurisdiction over, and provide effective criminal sanctions against, those persons who commit, or order to be committed, acts of intentional destruction of cultural heritage of great importance for humanity, whether or not it is inscribed on a list maintained by UNESCO or another international organization.[78]

However, '[d]ue to the weak and insubstantial content of its provisions ... this piece of legislation does not add anything significant to the international legal regulation of the phenomenon in discussion.'[79] This event highlighted to the international community that although the destruction of cultural heritage of great importance for humanity was already prohibited by international law, the international legal framework was *ad hoc*, 'fragmentary and mostly inductive.'[80] The then UNESCO Director General,

---

75 Marina Lostal, 'Syria's World Cultural Heritage and Individual Criminal Responsibility' (2015) 3 *International Review of Law* http://dx.doi.org/10.5339/irl.2015.3, 11, accessed 10 November 2019.
76 Francesco Badarin, 'Editorial' (2001) May–June *The World Heritage Newsletter* 1 and Francesco Francioni and Federico Lenzerini, 'The Destruction of the Buddhas of Bamiyan and International Law' (2003) 14 *European Journal of International Law* 610, 621; Marina Lostal, 'Syria's World Cultural Heritage and Individual Criminal Responsibility' (2015) 3 *International Review of Law* http://dx.doi.org/10.5339/irl.2015.3, 11, accessed 10 November 2019.
77 UNESCO Doc., WHC-01/CONF.208.23. Marina Lostal, 'Syria's World Cultural Heritage and Individual Criminal Responsibility' (2015) 3 *International Review of Law* http://dx.doi.org/10.5339/irl.2015.3, 11, accessed 10 November 2019.
78 Article VII, UNESCO Declaration concerning the Intentional Destruction of Cultural Heritage, adopted at Paris, 17 October 2003.
79 Federico Lenzerini, 'Terrorism, Conflicts and the Responsibility to Protect Cultural Heritage' (2016) 51(2) *The International Spectator* 70, 75.
80 Federico Lenzerini, 'Terrorism, Conflicts and the Responsibility to Protect Cultural Heritage' (2016) 51(2) *The International Spectator* 70, 75.

Koichiro Matsuura, stated that the destruction of the Buddhas required an investigation of 'all the means available to prevent and punish crimes against cultural properties within other existing convention.'[81] This led the Chair of the World Heritage Committee to declare that the destruction of the Buddhas illustrated that 'the application of the 1972 World Heritage Convention need[ed] to be reviewed to give it more "teeth" to deal with wanton destruction of World Heritage.'[82]

Lostal comments that '[t]he increase in the prospects of criminal accountability has been a driving force behind the adoption of international laws for the protection of cultural heritage.'[83] However, it is clear that gaps remain in the legal framework. The statutes of international criminal tribunals have sought to fill these gaps by including provisions on individual criminal responsibility, and the tribunals themselves have developed the discussion on the rationales for the protection of cultural heritage.

The ICTY and the destruction of cultural heritage

Cultural heritage was a significant victim of the Balkan Wars in the 1990s, as attempts were made to eradicate the cultural identity of ethnic groups by attacking their religious sites and cultural sites. It is during these conflicts that we witness a significant shift from damage done to cultural heritage as a result of collateral damage to the deliberate targeting of cultural heritage as a symbol of identity. Article 3(d) of the Statute of the International Criminal Tribunal for the Former Yugoslavia (ICTY) includes among the violations of the laws or customs of war in respect of which the Tribunal has jurisdiction 'seizure of, destruction or wilful damage done to institutions dedicated to religion, charity and education, the arts and sciences, historic monuments and works of art and science.'[84] The Statute thus took a 'civilian use' approach to the protection of cultural heritage. In practice, however, the Tribunal illustrated a much more expansive view of cultural heritage and highlighted the inextricable link between a people and its culture. In the case of *Prosecutor v Kordić and Čerzek*, for example, the

---

81 Francesco Badarin, 'Editorial' (2001) May–June *The World Heritage Newsletter* 1.
82 UNESCO Heritage Centre, 'Interview with Peter King, Chair of the World Heritage Committee' (2001) May-June *World Heritage Newsletter* 2 http://whc.unesco.org/doc uments/publi_news_30_en.pdf accessed 10 November 2019.
83 Marina Lostal, 'Syria's World Cultural Heritage and Individual Criminal Responsibility' (2015) 3 *International Review of Law* http://dx.doi.org/10.5339/irl.2015.3, 16, accessed 10 November 2019.
84 Statute of the International Criminal Tribunal of the Former Yugoslavia as established by Security Council Resolution 827 (1993).

26 Traditional paradigms

Tribunal found that destruction of places of worship amounted to 'an attack on the very religious identity of a people,'[85] citing the International Military Tribunal,[86] previous jurisprudence of the ICTY,[87] and the 1991 International Law Commission Report[88] in support of its designation of the destruction of religious buildings 'as a clear case of persecution as a crime against humanity.'[89] Regarding the destruction of religious buildings, the Chamber commented that

> This act, when perpetrated with the requisite discriminatory intent, amounts to an attack on the very religious identity of a people. As such, it manifests a nearly pure expression of the notion of 'crimes against humanity', for all of humanity is indeed injured by the destruction of a unique religious culture and its concomitant cultural objects. The Trial Chamber therefore finds that the destruction and wilful damage of institutions dedicated to Muslim religion or education, coupled with the requisite discriminatory intent, may amount to an act of persecution.[90]

In a similar vein, in the case of *Kristić*, the Tribunal found that the destruction of mosques underlined an attempt to erase the identity of the group and, as such, constituted 'evidence of an intent to physically destroy the group.'[91] In respect of the destruction of cultural heritage in the former Yugoslavia, the International Court of Justice (ICJ) agreed with the ICTY and affirmed that such destruction may indicate evidence of existence of the intent to commit genocide, although it is not categorised as genocide itself.[92]

---

85 *Prosecutor v Kordić and Čerzek*, IT-95-14/2-A, Trial Chamber Judgment, 26 February 2001, para. 206.
86 Nuremberg Judgment, *France and ors v Göring (Hermann) and ors*, Judgment and Sentence, [1946] 22 IMT 203, (1946) 41 AJIL 172, (1946) 13 ILR 203, ICL 243 (IMTN 1946), 1 October 1946, International Military Tribunal, 248, 302.
87 *Prosecutor v Blaškic*, IT-95-14, Trial Judgment, 3 March 2000, para. 227.
88 International Law Commission Report (1991) *Yearbook of the International Law Commission* 268. This states that persecution may take the form of the 'systematic destruction of monuments or buildings representative of a particular social, religious, cultural or other group' and also that '[p]ersecution may take many different forms, for example ... the systematic destruction of buildings or monuments representative of a particular social, religious, cultural or other group.'
89 *Prosecutor v Kordić and Čerzek*, IT-95-14/2-A, para. 206.
90 Ibid., para. 207.
91 *Prosecutor v Kristić*, IT-98-33-T, Trial Chamber Judgment, 2 August 2001, para. 508.
92 *Bosnia & Herzegovina v Serbia & Montenegro* [2007] ICJ 2, 244; ICJ, *Croatia v Serbia*, 390.

Thus, attacks against cultural heritage have been viewed as acts of persecution and as evidence of genocide by the ICTY, not just as war crimes as envisioned by its Statute, thereby illustrating both a 'civilian use' and 'culture-value' approach to its protection.

The ICC and the *Al Mahdi* case

Under Article 8(2)(b)(ix) of the Rome Statute, '[i]ntentionally directing attacks against buildings dedicated to religion, education, art, science or charitable purposes, historic monuments, hospitals and places where the sick and wounded are collected, provided they are not military objectives'[93] in an international armed conflict is a war crime. Article 8(2)(e)(iv) of the Statute also criminalises such attacks as war crimes in non-international armed conflicts.[94] Echoing the ICTY Statute, this illustrates a 'civilian use' paradigm of cultural heritage. However, the protection of cultural heritage was discussed in a more expansive way in the case of *Al Mahdi*.[95]

Al Mahdi was charged under Article 8(2)(e)(iv) of the Rome Statute with intentionally directing attacks against religious and historic monuments in Timbuktu, Mali, between 19 June 2012 and 10 July 2012, during which time numerous UNESCO World Heritage sites, including mausoleums and mosques, were targeted, damaged, and destroyed. *Al Mahdi* was the first case before the ICC which focused on the destruction of cultural property, and indeed, the first case before an international criminal tribunal which had the destruction of cultural property as the sole charge. Al Mahdi was a member of Ansar Dine, a mainly Tuareg movement associated with Al Qaeda in the Islamic Maghreb (AQIM). Until September 2012, he was the head of the *Hisbah* in Mali, a body set up to uphold public morals, which was responsible for the razing of numerous historic religious sites in Timbuktu, many of which were listed on the UNESCO World Heritage List.[96] The Pre-Trial Chamber found that the aim of the *Hisbah* was 'to prevent apparent vice and to promote virtue as well as to carry out charitable tasks'[97] and that the organisation was tasked with 'the prevention of anything that can be considered as worshipping the tombs, such as building

---

93 Article 8(2)(b)(ix) Statute of the International Criminal Court (1998), 2187 UNTS 90.
94 Article 8(2)(e)(iv) Statute of the International Criminal Court (1998), 2187 UNTS 90.
95 *Prosecutor v Al Mahdi*, ICC-01/12-01/15.
96 UNESCO's World Heritage Convention Nomination Documentation. See http://whc.unesco.org/en/nominations/ accessed 10 November 2019.
97 *Prosecutor v Al Mahdi*, ICC-01/12-01/15, 24 March 2016, ICC, Pre-Trial Chamber I, Decision on the confirmation of charges against Ahmad Al Faqi Al Mahdi, ICC-01/12-01/15, www.icc-cpi.int/CourtRecords/CR2016_02424.PDF accessed 10 April 2019, para. 46.

28 *Traditional paradigms*

the dome over the tomb.'[98] In June 2012, the leader of Ansar Dine, Iyad Ag Ghaly, after discussion with other Islamic leaders, decided to destroy the religious sites in Mali[99] because veneration of such sites conflicted with the fundamentalist view of Islam espoused by Ansar Dine. Al Mahdi[100] originally advised against destroying the mausoleums in order to preserve a good relationship between Ansar Dine and the local community,[101] but he subsequently carried out Ag Ghaly's orders to destroy the religious sites and he wrote a sermon on the destruction of the mausoleums to be read out at Friday prayer.[102] In this, he stated that the destruction of the domes had been ordered by 'le Messager' and that the destruction was not prohibited by religious sources.[103] Al Mahdi was involved in the destruction of some religious sites directly, and he oversaw the destruction of other sites.[104] The sites destroyed were the Sidi Mahamoud Ben Omar Mohamed Aquit Mausoleum, the Sheikh Mohamed Mahmoud Al Arawani Mausoleum,[105] the Sheik Sidi El Mokhtar Ben Sidi Mouhammad Al Kabir Al Kounti Mausoleum,[106] the Alpha Moya Mausoleum,[107] the Sheik Mouhamad El Mikki Mausoleum,[108] the Sheik Abdoul Kassim Attouaty Mausoleum,[109] the Sheik Sidi Ahmed Ben Amar Arragadi Mausoleum,[110] the door of the Sidi Yahia Mosque,[111] and the Bahaber Babadié Mausoleum and the Ahmed Fulane Mausoleum, both adjoining the Djingareyber Mosque.[112] All of the

---

98 Ibid., para. 47.
99 Agreement, ICC-01/12-01/15-78-Anx1-tENG-Red, para. 38.
100 Ibid., paras. 24, 38–40.
101 Ibid., para. 37.
102 Ibid., para. 44.
103 Ibid.
104 Ibid., para. 51. The Pre-Trial Chamber stated: 'In addition to the role played by Ahmad Al Faqi Al Mahdi in the administrative structures … [he] personally participated in or assisted to the material execution of the destruction of several Buildings/Structures. He participated in some instances using a pickaxe and was involved in the destructions at all four cemeteries concerned by supervising the work, giving advice, and 'preparing drinks and supervising the work, as well as providing the tools … including the pickaxes.' He provided the means for the destruction of the door at the Sidi Yahia Mosque and contributed in pulling out the door, and finally approved of the destruction of the domes adjacent to the Djingareyber Mosque, in which he participated himself at the beginning using a pickaxe, and later approved the use of a bulldozer.'
105 Agreement, ICC-01/12-01/15-78-Anx1-tENG-Red, paras. 64–65.
106 Ibid., paras. 66–72.
107 Ibid., paras. 73–78.
108 Ibid., paras. 85–86.
109 Ibid., paras. 87–88.
110 Ibid., paras. 82–84.
111 Ibid., paras. 89–95.
112 Ibid., paras. 96–103.

sites, bar one, were classified as World Heritage sites and protected by the UNESCO 1972 Convention on the Protection of the World Cultural and Natural Heritage.[113]

An arrest warrant was issued for Al Mahdi on 18 September 2015, and he was surrendered to the ICC on 26 September 2015. In March 2016, during the Confirmation of Charges Hearing, Al Mahdi let known his intention to plead guilty. His trial was speedily completed between 22 and 24 August 2016,[114] during which he made an admission of guilt. The Judgment was issued on 27 September 2016, with Al Mahdi being sentenced to nine years in prison.[115]

In the Confirmation of Charges Decision, the Pre-Trial Chamber stated that the buildings which had been targeted as part of Ansar Dine's campaign were part of the cultural heritage of Timbuktu and of Mali and that they did not constitute military objectives.[116] What is very interesting about this Decision is the way in which the destruction of cultural heritage is discussed and analysed, not just as a civilian objective but also as symbolic of the culture of the people of Timbuktu and of value to humanity as a whole. For example, the Prosecutor herself, commenting on the demolition of the religious buildings, commented that '[t]he destruction of such monuments constitutes the annihilation of structures that had survived the ravages of time and which stood as testimony to Timbuktu's glorious past and important place in history and to its people over generations.'[117] The Chamber took a similar approach in its Judgement, recalling the testimony of a UNESCO expert that 'the entire international community, in the belief that heritage is part of cultural life, is suffering as a result of the destruction of the protected sites.'[118] The Chamber thus concluded that the targeted sites were not simply religious buildings 'but had also a symbolic and emotional

---

113 UNESCO's World Heritage Convention Nomination Documentation, MLI-OTP-0004-0321; UNESCO's World heritage sites in Mali, MLI-OTP-0013-3630, 3715-26; Report of the World Heritage Committee, MLI-OTP-0006-3298, 3314.
114 ICC-01/12-01/15-T-4-Red-ENG, ICC-01/12-01/15-T-5-Red-ENG, ICC-01/12-01/15-T-6-ENG.
115 *The Prosecutor v Al Mahdi*, Verdict and Sentence, ICC-01/12-01/15-171, 27 September 2016.
116 Decision on the confirmation of charges against Ahmad Al Faqi Al Mahdi, ICC-01/12-01/15, 24 March 2016.
117 Statement of the Prosecutor of the International Criminal Court, Fatou Bensouda, at the opening of the confirmation of charges hearing in the case against Mr Ahmad Al Faqi Al Mahdi, 1 March 2016.
118 *The Prosecutor v Al Mahdi*, Verdict and Sentence, ICC-01/12-01/15-171, 27 September 2016, para. 80.

value for the inhabitants of Timbuktu' and that this was 'relevant in assessing the gravity of the crime committed.'[119]

Considerable discussion and analysis of the value of cultural heritage was undertaken during the Reparations phase of the *Al Mahdi* case. In the Reparations Order, issued on 17 August 2017, the Chamber found that Al Mahdi was liable for (a) the damage caused by the attack on nine mosques and the Sidi Yahia Mosque door; (b) the economic loss caused to the individuals whose livelihoods were contingent on the tourism and maintenance of these 'Protected Buildings' and to the community of Timbuktu as a whole; and (c) the moral harm resulting from the attacks. UNESCO, supported by other stakeholders, has now rebuilt or restored the sites which had been attacked in Timbuktu[120] at a cost of over €2.53 million,[121] and the Chamber calculated, based on witness reports, that Al Mahdi's liability was €97,000 in respect of the Protected Buildings.[122] The Chamber assessed Al Mahdi to be responsible for €2.12 million in respect of consequential economic loss. Finally, while highlighting the inherent difficulty in allocating a monetary measure for moral harm, the Chamber set his liability in this category at €483,000.[123] Al Mahdi's total liability, therefore, was assessed to be €2.7 million.[124] The Chamber, however, recognised that he was incapable of paying the reparations.[125] Throughout the Reparations decision, the Chamber focused on the impact of the destruction of the cultural heritage on the culture and people on Timbuktu. According to Balta and Banteka, the decision 'demonstrates respect for the culture of the victims, and by providing reparations, the Court created precedent for protecting the spiritual and religious connection between the victimized communities and protected buildings.'[126]

The Chamber required that '[t]o every extent possible, these reparations must be implemented in a gender and culturally sensitive manner.'[127] As part of the Reparations Order, the Chamber awarded nominal symbolic damages of €1 to the Malian State for the harm suffered due to the destruction of

---

119 Ibid., para. 79.
120 UNESCO Submissions, ICC-01/12-01/15-194, para. 12.
121 *Prosecutor v Al Mahdi*, Reparations Order, ICC-01/12-01/15, 17 August 2017, para. 116.
122 Ibid., para. 116.
123 Ibid., para. 133.
124 Ibid., para. 134.
125 Ibid., para. 113.
126 Alina Balta and Nadia Banteka, 'The Al-Mahdi Reparations Order at the ICC: A Step towards Justice for Victims of Crimes against Cultural Heritage' *Opinio Juris*, 6 September 2017.
127 *Prosecutor v Al Mahdi*, Reparations Order, ICC-01/12-01/15, 17 August 2017, para. 105.

Traditional paradigms 31

cultural heritage.[128] The Chamber also awarded a symbolic €1 to the international community, represented by UNESCO, in respect of the destruction of cultural heritage, as humanity as a whole had been impacted by Al Mahdi's actions in destroying cultural heritage.[129]

The issue of the damage caused by the destruction of cultural heritage was emphasised throughout the Reparations phase of this case. For example, in the Reparations Order, the Chamber held that victims had established two forms of moral harm to the requisite standard: '(i) mental pain and anguish, including losses of childhood, opportunities and relationships among those who fled Timbuktu because the Protected Buildings were attacked and (ii) disruption of culture.'[130] With regard to disruption of culture, the Chamber referred in a footnote to the fact that forms of moral harm caused by disruption of culture were recognised in international human rights law jurisprudence, and it referenced the cases of *Plan de Sánchez Massacre v Guatemala*[131] and *Yakye Axa Indigenous Community v Paraguay*,[132] which came before the Inter-American Court of Human Rights.[133] When addressing the harm emanating from the disruption of culture, the Chamber focused on a number of witness statements,[134] wherein witnesses commented on how the destruction of cultural heritage in Mali affected them emotionally. For example, one victim stated that 'I have never suffered so deeply in my life [...] Mentally, I was devastated. I felt humiliated by the destruction. I am still suffering [...] I am still affected mentally,'[135] while another commented that 'I lost everything with the destruction – my childhood, my belief and my attachment.'[136]

Section III of the Reparations Order focuses on the importance of international cultural heritage, with the Chamber stating that it was necessary 'to address the importance of cultural heritage, given that it is an essential component of the charges Mr Al Mahdi is convicted of.'[137] Recalling the testimony of one of the expert witnesses, the Chamber stated that 'cultural

---

128 Ibid., para. 106.
129 Ibid., para. 107.
130 Ibid., para. 85.
131 *Plan de Sánchez Massacre v Guatemala*, Judgment (Reparations), 19 November 2004, paras. 77, 85–88.
132 *Yakye Axa Indigenous Community v Paraguay*, Judgment (Merits, Reparations and Costs), 17 June 2005, paras. 154, 203.
133 *Prosecutor v Al Mahdi*, Reparations Order, ICC-01/12-01/15, 17 August 2017, para. 85.
134 Ibid., para. 85.
135 Cited in *Prosecutor v Al Mahdi*, Reparations Order, ICC-01/12-01/15, 17 August 2017, para. 85, submission a/35000/16, ICC-01/12-01/15-200-Conf-Anx5-Red-tENG, page 2.
136 Ibid.
137 *Prosecutor v Al Mahdi*, Reparations Order, ICC-01/12-01/15, 17 August 2017, para. 13.

32 Traditional paradigms

heritage plays a central role in the way communities define themselves and bond together, and how they identify with their past and contemplate their future.'[138]

It is thus clear that the ICC adopted a 'culture-value' approach to the destruction of cultural heritage in the *Al Mahdi* case, frequently emphasising the importance of heritage to group identity in addition to the emotional wellbeing of individuals. It also underscored the value of heritage to the international community and highlighted its contribution to humanity as a whole. This approach diverges significantly from the approach taken to cultural heritage in the text of the Rome Statute, which, as stated above, takes a 'civilian use' approach to its protection. The Court did not consider the destruction of cultural heritage under the framework of crimes against humanity or genocide, although originally the Prosecutor undertook an investigation into both war crimes and crimes against humanity in Mali, but only proceeded with war crimes charges.[139] It will be interesting to see how crimes in respect of cultural heritage will be dealt with at the Court in the future, given the expansive approach to this topic taken in the *Al Mahdi* case. Currently, the case of *Al Hassan*[140] is at the pre-trial stage before the Court. Al Hassan is an alleged member of Ansar Dine and *de facto* head of the Islamic police. He is charged with a number of crimes against humanity and war crimes, including directing attacks against buildings dedicated to religion and historic monuments. However, while the ICTY discussed attacks on cultural heritage under the frameworks of crimes against humanity and genocide, in addition to a war crimes framework, this may not be the case with the ICC. Indeed, the Chamber commented that 'the jurisprudence of the ICTY is of limited guidance given that, in contrast to the Statute, its applicable law does not govern "attacks" against cultural objects but rather punishes their "destruction or wilful damage". The legal contexts thus differ.'[141]

Nevertheless, the broader understanding of attacks on cultural heritage is to be preferred to the very narrow 'civilian use' approach incorporated into the text of the ICC Statute, and the discussion on the protection of cultural heritage in the *Al Mahdi* case was significant. Jakubowski comments that

---

138 Ibid., para. 14.
139 The Office of the Prosecutor, *Situation in Mali* Art. 53(1) Report, 16 January 2013, at 128.
140 *The Prosecutor v Al Hassan Ag Abdoul Aziz Ag Mohamed Ag Mahmoud*, ICC-01/12-01/18.
141 Situation in the Republic of Mali in the Case of *The Prosecutor v Ahmad Al Faqi Al Mahdi*, Judgment and Sentence, No.: ICC-01/12-01/15, 27 September 2016, para. 16.

[i]t … has been perceived as a landmark case, paving the way for a more efficient enforcement of international justice with respect to cultural heritage crimes. It has also served to enhance public awareness concerning the seriousness and gravity of international cultural heritage crimes for all humankind.[142]

In a similar vein, Luck comments that '[t]he al-Mahdi verdict certainly was an important step for justice and accountability, as well as an affirmation of the gravity of assaults on cultural heritage under international law.'[143]

While the case shone a spotlight on the destruction of cultural heritage and underlined the importance of culture in various facets of human life, and is thus very significant in the current discourse on the protection of cultural heritage, the ICC will not be the forum 'for executing justice in respect of cultural heritage crimes.'[144] It is doubtful if many cases in respect of cultural heritage will make their way before the court, and indeed, with regard to the recent spate of destruction of cultural heritage in Iraq and Syria, neither of these States have ratified the Rome Statute. In the case of *Al Mahdi*, the Chamber stated that the sentence would have 'a deterrent effect on others tempted to carry out similar acts in Mali or elsewhere.'[145] While it is hoped this may be the case, it is incumbent on States to take the primary responsibility to prosecute crimes against culture before their respective domestic courts.[146] It is suggested that the broader approach used by the ICTY, and indeed by the ICC in the *Al Mahdi* case, should be followed in future international and domestic cases concerning crimes against culture in order to reflect the importance of cultural heritage to humanity. Chapter 2 will further discuss the option of utilising a genocide framework for the prosecution of crimes against culture.

---

142 Andrzej Jakubowski, 'Resolution 2347: Mainstreaming the Protection of Cultural Heritage at the Global Level' (2018) 48 *Questions of International Law* 21, 28.
143 Edward C Luck, 'Cultural Genocide and the Protection of Cultural Heritage', J Paul Getty Trust Occasional Papers in Cultural Heritage Policy, Number 2 (2018), 12.
144 Andrzej Jakubowski, 'Resolution 2347: Mainstreaming the Protection of Cultural Heritage at the Global Level' (2018) 48 *Questions of International Law* 21, 28.
145 Jason Burke, 'ICC Ruling for Timbuktu Destruction "Should be Deterrent to Others"', *The Guardian*, 27 September 2016.
146 Andrzej Jakubowski, 'Resolution 2347: Mainstreaming the Protection of Cultural Heritage at the Global Level' (2018) 48 *Questions of International Law* 21, 29.

Conclusion

This chapter has outlined the multifarious legal instruments which seek to protect cultural heritage from attack during armed conflict. While such instruments are many and numerous, they have not been very successful in the protection of such heritage, and in no way stemmed the attacks on cultural heritage by the Islamic State of Iraq and Syria (ISIS) and other groups in their recent attacks on sites in Syria, Iraq, Mali, and Yemen.[147] The legal framework is unwieldy and *ad hoc*, and, as Lostal comments,

> The multiplication of treaties concerned with the protection of cultural heritage in times of armed conflict has created a multi-layered, multiconceptual field, afflicted by legislative congestion. Although they all presumably share a common purpose, each new convention fails to build upon its predecessors, and as a result, the field continues to develop on a piecemeal basis without a preconceived, systematic legislative plan.[148]

While it is clear that the extant legal framework is indeed disparate and complex, that is not to say that it has not garnered some successes. Recently, Serbia assumed responsibility for violations of the First Protocol to the 1954 Hague Convention during an armed conflict with Croatia, committed by its predecessor, the Federal Republic of Yugoslavia. In March 2012, both States signed an instrument which provided for the restitution by Serbia of certain cultural assets seized and removed from the territory of Croatia during the wars in the 1990s.[149] In addition, at the Eritrea-Ethiopia Claims Commission, which was set up to settle disputes between these two States emanating from events which happened during the war of 1998-2000,[150]

---

147 Jakubowski comments: 'Notwithstanding the wide recognition of the international obligations to protect cultural heritage from destruction and plunder in armed conflicts, such properties are still subject to attacks and looting. The destruction of the protected monuments in Timbuktu (Mali) in 2013 and the ongoing tragedy of historical and cultural heritage in Syria and Iraq are the most shocking examples of the failure to comply with the international law rules in this regard.' Ibid., 24.
148 Marina Lostal, *International Cultural Heritage Law in Armed Conflict* (Cambridge University Press 2017), 48.
149 Protocol on Restitution of Cultural Assets from Serbia to Croatia (signed 23 March 2012) https://www.tportal.hr/vijesti/clanak/protocol-on-restitution-of-cultural-assets-from-serbia-to-croatia-signed-20120323 accessed 19 February 2019.
150 Agreement between the Government of the State of Eritrea and the Government of the Federal Democratic Republic of Ethiopia (signed 12 December 2000, entered into force on the date of signature) UN Doc A/55/686-S/2000/1183 Annex.

Ethiopia was found responsible for the destruction of an important archaeological monument in Eritrea. This finding was made even though neither State was a party to the 1954 Hague Convention. Nevertheless, it was held that such an act 'was a violation of customary international humanitarian law'[151] and Ethiopia was required to pay compensation.[152] Indeed, UNESCO has underlined the potential of the current legal instruments in this sphere. It convened an international conference on Heritage and Cultural Diversity at Risk in Iraq and Syria on 3 December 2014, at which it called for the implementation of the 1954 Hague Convention for the Protection of Cultural Property in the Event of Armed Conflict. However, as noted by Cuno,

> [r]egardless of the Convention's good intentions, given the chaos and existential threats the two nations currently face, it is difficult to imagine Iraq and Syria filling out the forms and making the case for enhanced protection of the many cultural heritage sites and monuments within their jurisdiction. It is equally difficult to imagine ISIS intimidated or rebuffed by such enhanced protection if it were provided to Iraq and Syria.[153]

Indeed, despite the existence of numerous instruments on prohibiting attacks on cultural heritage, the 'problem has been getting worse in recent years.'[154]

Therefore, a new paradigm on the protection of cultural heritage is needed. This chapter has illustrated that the extant legal framework has been built on both the 'civilian use' and 'culture-value' paradigms. The next chapter identifies newer paradigms in the discourse on the protection of cultural heritage, and explores the potential efficacy of the inter-related concepts of cultural cleansing, the Responsibility to Protect doctrine, and cultural genocide to increase its protection.

---

151 Partial Award – Central Front – Eritrea's Claims 2, 4, 6, 7, 8 and 22 (28 April 2004) https://arbitrationlaw.com/library/eritrea-ethiopia-claims-commission-partial-awards-central-front-eritreas-clains-2-4-6-7-8-22 para. 113.
152 Ibid., para. 114.
153 James Cuno, 'The Responsibility to Protect the World's Cultural Heritage' (2016) 23 *Brown J World Affairs* 97, 102.
154 Edward C Luck, 'Cultural Genocide and the Protection of Cultural Heritage', J Paul Getty Trust Occasional Papers in Cultural Heritage Policy, Number 2 (2018), 12.

2 Potential paradigms
Cultural cleansing, the Responsibility to Protect doctrine and cultural genocide

Introduction

As stated in the Introduction to this book, the former Director General of the United Nations Educational, Scientific and Cultural Organization (UNESCO), Irina Bokova, frequently and consistently employed the term 'cultural cleansing' to describe attacks on cultural heritage undertaken by fundamentalist Islamic groups such as the Islamic State of Iraq and Syria (ISIS) and Ansar Dine in the Middle East and Africa while she was in office.[1] While this term pre-dates the recent conflicts discussed,[2] it has been utilised recurrently in respect of these conflicts by both policy makers and academics.[3] Bokova's choice of this emotive and evocative term in the context of the recent attacks on Syria and Iraq is significant. Utilising cultural cleansing instead of, for example, 'attacks on cultural property/heritage' focused attention on the fact that the destruction was more than collateral damage in an armed conflict context.

---

1 Irina Bokova, 'Culture on the Front Line of New Wars' (2015) 22 *Brown Journal of World Affairs* 289, 289. See also UNESCO, 'The Director-General of UNESCO calls for all Syrians to commit to the safeguarding of cultural heritage in Bosra and Idlib' http://whc.unesco.org/en/news/1257 accessed 10 November 2019; UNESCO, 'UNESCO Director-General Condemns Destruction at Nimrud' http://en.unesco.org/news/unesco-director-general-condemns-destruction-nimrud 10 November 2019.
2 The term 'cultural cleansing' was used prior to the recent spate of attacks on cultural heritage. Baker, Ismael, and Ismael use the term in the context of the intervention in Iraq – Raymond Baker, Shereen Ismael, and Tareq Ismael, *Cultural Cleansing in Iraq. Why Museums Were Looted, Libraries Burned and Academics Murdered* (Pluto Press, 2009).
3 See Edward C Luck, 'Cultural Genocide and the Protection of Cultural Heritage,' J Paul Getty Trust Occasional Papers in Cultural Heritage Policy, Number 2 (2018); James Cuno, 'The Responsibility to Protect the World's Cultural Heritage' (2016) 23 *Brown J World Affairs* 97.

In 2015, Bokova described her understanding of cultural cleansing, stating that

> [i]n Iraq and Syria, we are witnessing what can be described as cultural cleansing on an unprecedented scale. This cultural cleansing is an attack on cultural diversity that combines the destruction of monuments and the persecution of people. In today's new conflicts, these two dimensions cannot be separated. Violent extremism attacks human rights and dignity, seeking to destroy diversity and freedom in order to impose sectarian visions, a core aim of many of the new organizations rising up in different parts of the world, on societies that have always featured rich diversity, exchange, and dialogue across cultures.[4]

The essence of cultural cleansing is thus that it is not just the physical structure or cultural site that is destroyed, but rather an aspect of identity, of history, of memory of 'the Other.' The destruction of cultural heritage is now a strategy of war, with the objective being to eliminate cultural diversity and pluralism, 'erase all sources of belonging and identity, and destroy the fabric of society.'[5] Such acts have long-lasting and far-reaching impacts on society as they facilitate the replacement of cultural diversity with homogeneity. Thus, the societal structures in the locales of attacks on cultural sites are changed irrevocably, potentially leading to 'social disintegration'.[6] Such attacks can result in social and cultural engineering, in addition to causing emotional and psychological harm to members of the group whose culture has been attacked. By targeting sites and artefacts of cultural significance to a particular group, the group's identity can be eroded. Such attacks eliminate 'the layers of history, cities, and homes affects people's perceptions of the past and present and shadows their confidence in a future where their rights and dignity would be respected.'[7] Therefore, Bokova comments, the protection of culture should no longer been viewed as a luxury 'to be left for another day', but rather the need to protect culture is immediate.[8]

Bokova's use of the term 'cultural cleansing' served to attract global attention to the events that were unfolding in the Middle East and in Africa. Rather than 'mere' buildings and monuments being damaged, which may not have had an impact on many people outside of those with a direct interest

---

4 Irina Bokova, 'Culture on the Front Line of New Wars' (2015) 22(1) *Brown Journal of World Affairs* 289, 289.
5 Ibid., 290.
6 Ibid., 291.
7 Ibid.
8 Ibid., 294.

38 *Potential paradigms*

in archaeology or history, UNESCO, via Bokova, emphasised the fact that much more was being lost in the form of group memory, identity and cultural diversity. The description of the acts as cultural cleansing also highlighted that damage was being done to the societal foundations in Iraq and Syria, thus garnering international attention. This term was subsequently used in the media and by other policy and academic commentators in the context of the destruction of cultural heritage in the Middle East and Africa.

Attacks on cultural heritage have de-escalated somewhat recently, and it also seems that the term cultural cleansing has recently lost some of its popularity. Bokova is no longer the Director General of UNESCO, and the phrase has not been employed in high-level policy meetings on cultural heritage. While the phrase may have lost some of its cachet in recent times, its use was an valuable tool in focusing the world's attention on the true implications of the destruction of cultural sites and artefacts, in educating the global community on the role of culture in society, and in alerting States to take measures in respect of the safeguarding of cultural property. However, the value of using the term cultural cleansing from a legal perspective is unclear. As seen in the previous chapter, attacks on cultural heritage can constitute war crimes if committed in the context of an armed conflict, and can potentially be prosecuted by the International Criminal Court (ICC). In addition, it may be viewed as a crime against humanity if the focus is placed on the persecution element of the destruction, and furthermore it may also be viewed as evidence of intention to commit genocide, given the jurisprudence of the International Criminal Tribunal for the Former Yugoslavia (ICTY). However, there is no international crime of cultural cleansing. This chapter will, therefore, assess the efficacy of using the cultural cleansing label from a legal perspective in respect of attacks on cultural heritage. In addition, it will also focus on recent attempts to apply the Responsibility to Protect (R2P) framework to situations of cultural cleansing, as has been done in the case of ethnic cleansing. Finally, it will address the issue of cultural genocide, to ascertain if the recent acts of violence against cultural heritage could fall under the crime of genocide. The first section focuses on the concept of cultural cleansing, while the second addresses the relationship between cultural cleansing and the R2P doctrine. The final section then analyses the related issue of cultural genocide.

What is 'cultural cleansing'?

Petrovic highlights that a number of conflicts since the end of the Cold War have been hallmarked by attacks on cultural heritage and the denial of the Other by such means, and comments that '[i]n its more grotesque form, it is not only about destroying people's identity, self, and personhood, as well as physical bodies, as strategic targets of armed conflict, but also about "what military strategists conceive of as humanity".[9] In a similar vein, Nordstrom comments that '[s]elf and identity constitute the hidden casualties of war.'[10]

The concept of cultural cleansing is related to that of ethnic cleansing. The latter concept, which came to the fore in the Balkan Wars of the 1990s, has been described as 'a journalistic expression derived from Serbian propaganda' which 'was soon incorporated into common political language.'[11] The acts which constituted ethnic cleansing were discussed in the final report of the Commission of Experts, which was set up to investigate crimes committed on the territory of the former Yugoslavia.[12] However, the concept remains vague with imprecise contours, with some commentators considering it to be another label for genocide, while others view it as distinct from genocide as its aim is to displace, rather than destroy, ethnic groups.[13] Ethnic cleansing is not recognised as an international crime. It has, however, found a role in the international legal framework via the R2P doctrine. The question arises, therefore, if cultural cleansing could also trigger the application of this doctrine.

The R2P doctrine

The development of the R2P doctrine

The Responsibility to Protect 'embodies a political commitment to end the worst forms of violence and persecution.'[14] It was developed outside of the UN framework in response to the devastating conflicts in Rwanda and the Balkans in the 1990s. Following on from these conflicts and the much-criticised North Atlantic Treaty Organization (NATO) intervention in Kosovo,[15] in 1999 the then Secretary General of the United Nations (UN), Kofi Annan,

---

9 Jadranka Petrovic, 'The Cultural Dimension of Peace Operations: Peacekeeping and Cultural Property' in Andrew H Campbell (ed), *Global Leadership Initiatives in Conflict Resolution and Peacebuilding* (IGO Global 2018), 84, 85.
10 C Nordstrom, 'Terror Warfare and the Medicine of Peace' (1998) 12(1) *Medical Anthropology Quarterly* 103, 105.
11 Elise Novic, *The Concept of Cultural Genocide* (Oxford University Press 2016), 46.
12 UNSC, 'Final Report of the Commission of Experts Established Pursuant to Security Council Resolution 780 (1992)' (27 May 1994) UN Doc S/1994/674. See Elise Novic, *The Concept of Cultural Genocide* (Oxford University Press 2016), 46.
13 Elise Novic, *The Concept of Cultural Genocide* (Oxford University Press 2016), 46–47.
14 United Nations Office on Genocide Prevention and the Responsibility to Protect, 'Responsibility to Protect' https://www.un.org/en/genocideprevention/about-responsibilit y-to-protect.shtml accessed 10 November 2019.
15 See Benjamin Lambert, *NATO's Air War for Kosovo: A Strategic and Operational Assessment* (Rand 2001).

40 Potential paradigms

challenged UN member States to 'find common ground in upholding the principles of the Charter, and acting in defence of common humanity.'[16] He reiterated this challenge the following year in his Millennium Report, questioning that 'if humanitarian intervention is, indeed, an unacceptable assault on sovereignty, how should we respond to a Rwanda, to a Srebrenica, to gross and systematic violation of human rights that offend every precept of our common humanity?'[17] In response to this question, the International Commission on Intervention and State Sovereignty (ICISS), which was established by the Canadian government, issued a report titled *The Responsibility to Protect* in 2001.[18] This report revisits the concept of sovereignty and underlines that it does not just mean protection from interference from outside force; rather, sovereignty also requires States to take responsibility for the population under their control. Thus, the basic principle underlying the R2P doctrine has three main pillars: (1) the primary responsibility to protect its populations rests with the State; (2) the international community has a responsibility to assist the State in meeting this obligation; (3) but if a State is unwilling or unable to ensure such protection, then the international community has a responsibility to intervene by using appropriate diplomatic, humanitarian, and other peaceful means to protect the population. The international community must also be prepared to use stronger measures, including the collective use of force, in line with the UN Charter framework, if necessary. The scope of the R2P doctrine was limited to four areas, that is, genocide, war crimes, crimes against humanity, and ethnic cleansing. This is despite the fact that 'ethnic cleansing' is not a recognised international crime.

The R2P doctrine gradually made its way into the consciousness of the UN, and its underlying principle was endorsed in the report of the High Level Panel on Threats, Challenges and Change[19] in 2004 and in the

---

16 UN secretary general, Press Release SG/SM/7136, 20 September 1999; Ralph Steinke, 'A Look Back at NATO's 1999 Kosovo Campaign: A Questionably "Legal" but Justifiable Exception?' (2015) 14(4) *Connections* 43.
17 Kofi A Annan, 'We the Peoples. The Role of the United Nations in the 21st Century' (2000), 48 https://www.un.org/en/events/pastevents/pdfs/We_The_Peoples.pdf accessed 10 November 2019.
18 Report of the International Commission on Intervention and State Sovereignty (2001) http://responsibilitytoprotect.org/ICISS%20Report.pdf accessed 10 November 2019.
19 High Level Panel Report on Threats, Challenges and Change, 'A More Secure World: Our Shared Responsibility,' A/59/565 (2004). https://www.un.org/ruleoflaw/blog/document/the-secretary-generals-high-level-panel-report-on-threats-challenges-and-change-a-more-secure-world-our-shared-responsibility/ accessed 10 November 2019.

Secretary General's report *In Larger Freedom* in 2005.[20] Neither of these reports identified a basis to use force for the purposes of protection under the doctrine, apart from authorisation of the Security Council under Chapter VII of the UN Charter. Finally, in 2005, UN member States committed to the R2P doctrine by including it in the Outcome Document of the 2005 UN World Summit meeting,[21] in a somewhat recast formulation. While the basic elements of the doctrine are retained, some of the elements originally proposed in the ICISS Report were omitted. However, in paragraphs 138 and 139 of the World Summit Outcome Document, State leaders affirmed their responsibility to protect their own populations from genocide, war crimes, ethnic cleansing, and crimes against humanity and accepted a collective responsibility to encourage and facilitate each other in upholding this commitment. States also declared their readiness to take timely and decisive action to protect populations when national authorities are unwilling or unable to do so, in accordance with the UN Charter and in cooperation with relevant regional organizations.[22]

Given that the Outcome Document is a General Assembly Resolution, it – including paragraphs 138 and 139 – comprises a significant political commitment by States to live up to their extant international legal obligations to refrain from, and to prevent, acts of genocide, crimes against humanity, war crimes, and also ethnic cleansing. The doctrine

> offers fresh programmatic opportunities for the United Nations system to assist states in preventing the listed crimes and violations and in protecting affected populations through capacity building, early warning, and other preventive and protective measures, rather than simply waiting to respond if they fail.[23]

The doctrine has been referred to in a number of UN resolutions since its adoption by the organisation, and the UN has expanded the role States have

---

20 Report of the Secretary General, 'In Larger Freedom: Towards Development, Security and Human Rights for All,' A/59/2005 https://undocs.org/A/59/2005 accessed 10 November 2019.
21 World Summit Outcome Document, A/RES/60/1 (2005) https://www.un.org/en/developm ent/desa/population/migration/generalassembly/docs/globalcompact/A_RES_60_1.pdf accessed 10 November 2019.
22 Paras. 138 and 139, World Summit Outcome Document, A/RES/60/1 (2005) https://www.un.org/en/development/desa/population/migration/generalassembly/docs/globalcom pact/A_RES_60_1.pdf accessed 10 November 2019.
23 United Nations Office on Genocide Prevention and the Responsibility to Protect, 'Responsibility to Protect' https://www.un.org/en/genocideprevention/about-responsibilit y-to-protect.shtml accessed 10 November 2019.

42 Potential paradigms

in respect of implementing the doctrine on a number of occasions. In 2009, the Secretary General provided guidelines for the implementation of the doctrine,[24] in addition to additional guidelines on State responsibility.[25] In 2016, the Secretary General also set out a plan as to how best to mobilise for collective action over the following decade, which drew on R2P doctrine principles.[26] Luck comments that

> [t]he core thesis of the commission's report – that there is an international and national responsibility to protect populations from existential threats – has taken root and proven to be remarkably resilient. This speaks to how valuable the innovative and timely framing of an issue can be. Yet neither the theoretical construct nor few, if any, of the commission's recommendations have been accepted by the Member States.[27]

Nevertheless, the Security Council specifically referred to the R2P doctrine in Resolution 1973 in respect of Libya in 2011.[28] This resolution marked the first, and to date, only, explicit authorisation of the implementation of the doctrine by the Security Council. This resolution resulted in intervention in Libya by NATO and a number of key allies, which ultimately resulted in the downfall of the Ghaddafi regime. The R2P doctrine was strongly criticised in the aftermath of the Libyan intervention and its credibility was questioned,[29] being condemned as a political tool and justification for intervention by Western States because it was felt in some quarters that NATO went beyond permissible measures and was involved in regime change.[30]

---

24 UN Document, 'Report of the Secretary-General, Implementing the Responsibility to Protect,' A/63/677, 12 January 2009.
25 GA Res 67/929-S/2013/399 (9 July 2013).
26 GA Res 70/999-S/2016/620 (17 August 2016).
27 Edward C Luck, 'Cultural Genocide and the Protection of Cultural Heritage,' J Paul Getty Trust Occasional Papers in Cultural Heritage Policy, Number 2 (2018), 15.
28 SC Resolution 1973 (17 March 2011).
29 See, for example, David Rieff, 'REP, RIP,' *New York Times* (7 November 2011) http://www.nytimes.com/2011/11/08/opinion/r2p-rip.html accessed 10 November 2019.
30 See Sarah Brockmeier, Oliver Stuenkel, and Marcos Tourino, 'The Impact of the Libya Intervention Debates on Norms of Protection' (2016) 30(1) *Global Society* 134, 134. See also Francesco Francioni and Christine Bakker, 'Responsibility to Protect, Humanitarian Intervention and Human Rights: Lessons from Libya to Mali,' Transworld Working Paper No 15, (2013) https://www.iai.it/sites/default/files/TW_WP_15.pdf accessed 19 Februrary 2020.

The R2P doctrine and the protection of cultural heritage

In 2015, a journalist named Hugh Eakin wrote: 'While the United Nations has adopted the "responsibility to protect" ... doctrine, to allow for international intervention to stop imminent crimes of war or genocide, no such parallel principle has been introduced for cultural heritage.'[31] This marked the beginning of a still continuing discussion in academia and among civil society organisations, questioning if the R2P doctrine would be a suitable framework to improve the protection of cultural heritage.

UNESCO met in November 2015 to discuss potential responses to the recent destruction of cultural heritage as well as strategies for preserving cultural heritage sites. The organisation recommended, in part, that the R2P doctrine could be a useful framework for States to apply to prevent the further destruction of cultural heritage. This recommendation has since been taken up by international organisations and academics. For example, the American Academy of Arts and Sciences and the J Paul Getty Trust are currently working together to investigate how R2P may be applied to the protection of cultural heritage, and a number of international experts, some of whom have first-hand knowledge of the original R2P negotiations, met in London in November 2016 to explore this question further.[32] In respect of the issues faced in such discussions, Cuno states that

> [t]he question is simple: if states have the obligation to protect the cultural heritage within their borders, as the UN has repeatedly said that they do, what responsibility does the international community have when the state is unable or unwilling to exercise that obligation?[33]

Regarding the potential application of the doctrine of R2P to the destruction of cultural heritage, two questions arise. First, does the scope of R2P extend to the destruction of cultural heritage, and second, what is the likelihood of such an application?

In respect of the first question, it is important to note that former Secretary General Ban Ki-moon's 2009 report on the R2P doctrine warned against extending its scope, stating that to extend the doctrine to other issues such as HIV/AIDS, climate change, or natural disasters 'would undermine the 2005 consensus and stretch the concept beyond recognition and operational

---

31 Hugh Eakin, 'Use Force to Stop ISIS' Destruction of Art and History,' *New York Times* (3 April 2015).
32 James Cuno, 'The Responsibility to Protect the World's Cultural Heritage' (2016) 23 *Brown J World Affairs* 97, 105.
33 Ibid.

utility.'[34] Therefore, there is a clear intention not to expand the R2P framework to issues which were not seen as falling within its scope when it was adopted by the UN in 2005. However, as highlighted above, the R2P doctrine was enshrined in the UN framework as the '[r]esponsibility to protect populations from genocide, war crimes, ethnic cleansing and crimes against humanity.'[35] Therefore, the R2P doctrine could potentially be applied to the destruction of cultural property, if such destruction is identified as a war crime (which is the traditional approach taken in the legal framework) or a crime against humanity (if the destruction of cultural heritage were recognised as an act of persecution) or as an act of genocide (if, for example, cultural genocide were accepted as falling within the crime of genocide, a question which will be dealt with here). Technically, the R2P framework also applies to situations of ethnic cleansing. The frequent use of the term cultural cleansing by Bokova, echoing the concept of ethnic cleansing, may lead one to surmise that the latter is a form of the other, or at least that there is some overlap between the two. However, as neither concept has been legally defined, it is difficult to have certainty on this issue.

It is important to note that the R2P doctrine focuses on the protection of *populations*. In this context, the link between a people, its culture, and its identity needs to be recognised and acknowledged if the R2P framework is to be applicable. Unfortunately, the ICICSS report does not elaborate very much on the concept of culture. The report mentions how non-intervention should be prioritized when possible to 'protect peoples and cultures,'[36] but it does not address culture as being indivisible from the concept of a population, and thus, the question of whether the R2P doctrine is applicable to situations of cultural heritage destruction is left open to interpretation.

Lenzerini strongly supports the argument that the destruction of cultural heritage falls within the scope of the R2P doctrine, and opines that the third pillar of the doctrine places an obligation on the international community, via the Security Council, to intervene. He states that his conclusion is buttressed by the fact that cultural heritage represents a common interest of the international community as a whole, which implies an *erga omnes* obligation to act to protect it. He comments that

---

34 Secretary-General's address at event on 'Responsible Sovereignty: International Cooperation for a Changed World' (15 July 2008) https://www.un.org/sg/en/content/sg/statement/2008-07-15/secretary-generals-address-event-responsible-sovereignty accessed 10 July 2019.
35 GA Resolution 60/1, UN Doc A/RES/60/1 (24 October 2005), paras. 138–139.
36 Report of the International Commission on Intervention and States Sovereignty, 'The Responsibility to Protect' (2001) http://responsibilitytoprotect.org/ICISS%20Report.pdf accessed 10 November 2019, para. 4.11.

> [w]hen an obligation of this kind is involved, any state other than the state directly injured by a violation may take lawful measures to ensure cessation of the breach and reparation in the interest of the injured state or the beneficiaries of the obligation breached, as affirmed by Article 54 of the 2001 International Law Commission's Articles on Responsibility of States for Internationally Wrongful Acts.[37]

However, he points out that

> [w]hat is much more doubtful is whether unilateral action by states not authorised by the S[ecurity] C[ouncil] is possible, as several states cast doubts on its legality. Moreover, in the current state of international law, it cannot yet be maintained that an established rule of customary international law actually exists allowing states to implement the R2P doctrine through unauthorised unilateral military intervention outside their national borders.[38]

In reality, the UN frequently refrains from intervening in civil wars, even if they engender large-scale atrocities. However, Lenzerini comments that '[i]n consideration of the fundamental importance of the value protected, its correspondence to an *erga omnes* interest, and the scope of R2P, which goes beyond the traditional concept of Westphalian sovereignty, the inability by the SC to act should not prevent R2P from being put into practice.'[39] He points to recent practice of intervention without Security Council backing, including the French intervention in Mali in 2013; the joint offensive against Boko Haram in Nigeria by Benin, Cameroon, Chad, France, and Niger in 2014, which was followed by a Multinational Joint Task Force authorised to intervene by the African Union in 2015; and the actions by some States against Islamic State of Iraq and Syria (ISIS) in Iraq and Syria, which commenced before being explicitly authorised by the Security Council.

Clearly Lenzerini is a strong supporter of a potential move to implement the R2P doctrine in response to destruction of cultural heritage. He states that 'it is indispensable that the doctrine ... be put into practice seriously and effectively with the purpose of protecting humanity against the irreplaceable loss of its heritage.'[40] Luck also highlights a number of advan-

---

37 Federico Lenzerini, 'Terrorism, Conflicts and the Responsibility to Protect Cultural Heritage' (2016) 51(2) *The International Spectator* 70, 80.
38 Ibid., 81.
39 Ibid.
40 Ibid., 70.

tages of utilising the R2P framework in the context of cultural heritage, commenting that

> [s]ubstantively, R2P offers a ... mixed framework for thinking about how to protect cultural heritage. On the plus side, the notions of responsibility and protection are central to both tasks. That responsibility should be individual as well as collective, encompassing peoples, groups, civil society, and the private sector as well as governments and international institutions. Member States have been much readier to accept the preventive and assistance dimensions of R2P than those that might entail the use of force.[41]

The J Paul Getty Trust issued a report on cultural cleansing in 2017, which focused on the use of R2P as a method of protection of cultural heritage. In this document, Weiss and Connolly state that the application of the doctrine to destruction of cultural heritage is sensible for four reasons. First, they comment, the R2P framework formulated by ICISS, which includes three aspects: prevention, reaction, and rebuilding, 'employs the same standard vocabulary frequently applied to concerns about the protection of cultural heritage in war zones.'[42] Second, the R2P framework, which was remodelled after the UN's 2005 World Summit, can also be applied to the protection of cultural heritage given that it relies on three pillars put forward by then UN Secretary-General, Ban Ki-moon: the primary responsibility of the state for protection, the international responsibility to fortify that state capacity, and the international responsibility to respond in cases of egregious failure. Third, they identify the major obstacle in the way of action for the protection of people is the same as that for the protection of heritage, that is, sovereignty. Fourth, they comment that the 'protection of people and the protection of culture are inseparable; cultural heritage plays an important role in the restoration of civil society and the revitalization of local economies postconflict.'[43] Furthermore, Weiss and Connolly state that '[i]n any case, there is no need for a hierarchy of protection because the choice between the two is false, just as a choice between people and the natural environment is false. Air, water, and culture are essential for life.'[44]

---

41 Edward C Luck, 'Cultural Genocide and the Protection of Cultural Heritage,' J Paul Getty Trust Occasional Papers in Cultural Heritage Policy, Number 2 (2018), 15.
42 Thomas G Weiss and Nina Connelly, 'Cultural Cleansing and Mass Atrocities,' J Paul Getty Trust Occasional Papers, No. 1 (2017), 6.
43 Ibid.
44 Ibid.

Potential paradigms 47

While, in theory, there is much support for the application of the R2P doctrine to situations of cultural heritage destruction, it is unlikely that strong political support will be forthcoming. The use of the doctrine as a basis for the intervention in Libya in 2011 was heavily criticised, and it left a number of questions concerning its scope. The contours of the R2P doctrine are far from clear, and indeed, it is difficult to assert that the international community has universally accepted its full implementation.[45] Ultimately, Luck comments that '[t]here would be great resistance to extending R2P principles directly to the protection of cultural heritage.'[46] It is thus concluded that the R2P framework would not be an effective paradigm for dealing with the destruction of cultural heritage, at least until its legal status and contours have been more clearly defined and it has been definitively accepted by the international community of States.

Cultural genocide

The use of the term cultural cleansing and the suggestions to look to the R2P doctrine in the context of the protection of cultural heritage have awakened, to some degree, the related topic of cultural genocide. Given that the R2P framework can apply in situations of genocide, the question of whether the destruction of heritage can fall under the definition of genocide in international law has been posed. The scope of the crime of genocide has quite frequently been examined since the Genocide Convention was first debated at the UN in 1948.[47] While the definition of genocide has remained constant, with the definition in the Genocide Convention subsequently being replicated in a number of international criminal law statutes, including the Statute of the International Criminal Court, the question of whether or not the destruction of culture can constitute genocide has resurfaced periodically among commentators, most notably in the context of the rights of indigenous peoples, as well as in the aftermath of the Balkan Wars in the mid-1990s. The recent spate of attacks on cultural heritage in the Middle East and Africa seems to have reignited this analysis once again. The following section thus briefly retraces the drafting of the definition of the crime of genocide under international law, and assesses if the cultural

---

45 Edward C Luck, 'Cultural Genocide and the Protection of Cultural Heritage,' J Paul Getty Trust Occasional Papers in Cultural Heritage Policy, Number 2 (2018), 15.
46 Ibid.
47 Convention on the Prevention and Punishment of the Crime of Genocide, opened for signature 9 December 1948, 78 UNTS 277.

genocide paradigm is a suitable way in which to address destruction of cultural heritage.

The conceptualisation of genocide

While acts of genocide have been perpetrated throughout history, the crime of genocide is a new one, with the term being coined by Polish lawyer Raphael Lemkin in response to the Holocaust. The etymology of the term emanates from the Greek work *genos*, meaning *race* or *kind*, and the suffix *-cide* denoting an act of killing, from the Latin *caedere*, meaning *kill*. Lemkin had witnessed the Armenian genocide and had attempted for several years to find legal categorisations and definitions which would fit such actions. In 1933, he submitted a set of proposals to the Fifth International Conference for the Unification of Criminal Law, convened under the auspices of the League of Nations. The submission included a report and draft provisions on

> *barbarity*, conceived as oppressive and destructive acts directed against individuals as members of national, religious, or racial group, and the crime of *vandalism*, conceived as malicious destruction of works of art and culture because they represent the specific creations of the genius of such groups.[48]

From the proposals on vandalism, it is seen that Lemkin saw a clear connection between destruction of culture and destruction of a group. However, despite the contemporaneous events in Europe in 1933, neither of Lemkin's proposals were accepted by States. [49]

Lemkin originally propounded a broad definition of genocide, which included the destruction of culture as a technique of genocide.[50] Writing in 1944, he explained that

> Generally speaking, genocide does not necessarily mean the immediate destruction of a nation … It is intended … to signify a coordinated plan of different actions aiming at the destruction of essential foundations of the life of national groups, with the aim of annihilating the groups

---

48 Raphael Lemkin, *Axis Rule in Occupied Europe: Laws of Occupation, Analysis of Government, and Proposals for Redress* (Carnegie Endowment for International Peace 1944), 91, emphasis in original.
49 Edward C Luck, 'Cultural Genocide and the Protection of Cultural Heritage,' J Paul Getty Trust Occasional Papers in Cultural Heritage Policy, Number 2 (2018), 17.
50 Elise Novic, *The Concept of Cultural Genocide* (Oxford University Press 2016), 4.

Potential paradigms 49

themselves. The objectives of such a plan would be disintegration of the political and social institutions, of culture, language, national feelings, religion, and the economic existence of national groups, and the destruction of personal security, liberty, health, dignity, and even the lives of the individuals belonging to such groups. Genocide is directed against the national group as an entity, and the actions involved are directed against individuals, not in their individual capacity, but as members of the national group.[51]

In Lemkin's opinion, attacks on the culture of a group normally preceded and foreshadowed physical violence against the group. He echoed the thoughts of the 19th-century German Jewish poet Heinrich Heine, stating 'First they burn books and then they start burning bodies'.[52] Heine had commented in 1821, 'Where they have burned books, they will end in burning human beings.' In fact, Heine's works were among those burned on Berlin's Opernplatz in 1933, portending the Holocaust.[53] Dirk Moses quotes Lemkin as having asserted that 'physical and biological genocide are always preceded by cultural genocide or by an attack on the symbols of the group or by violent interference with religious or cultural activities.'[54] In Lemkin's view, the intent to destroy a group required the destruction of their way of life, because otherwise, the horrific task would be incomplete, and '[a]ttacks on culture ... usually came first.'[55] Lemkin thus 'saw genocide as a much more systematic and strategic crime, one with many dimensions and layers.'[56]

51 Raphael Lemkin, *Axis Rule in Occupied Europe: Laws of Occupation, Analysis of Government, and Proposals for Redress* (Carnegie Endowment for International Peace 1944), 79.
52 Donna-Lee Frieze (ed), *Totally Unofficial: The Autobiography of Raphael Lemkin* (Yale University Press 2013), 172.
53 See Edward C Luck, 'Cultural Genocide and the Protection of Cultural Heritage,' J Paul Getty Trust Occasional Papers in Cultural Heritage Policy, Number 2 (2018), 4 – Foreword by James Cuno.
54 A Dirk Moses, 'Raphael Lemkin, Culture and the Concept of Genocide', in Donald Bloxham and A Dirk Moses (eds) *The Oxford Handbook of Genocide Studies* (Oxford University Press 2010), 34.
55 Donna-Lee Frieze (ed), Totally Unofficial: The Autobiography of Raphael Lemkin (Yale University Press 2013), 172.
56 Edward C Luck, 'Cultural Genocide and the Protection of Cultural Heritage,' J Paul Getty Trust Occasional Papers in Cultural Heritage Policy, Number 2 (2018), 20.

50 *Potential paradigms*

Genocide as an international crime

In the aftermath of World War II, the Holocaust, and the subsequent prosecutions at Nuremberg, the newly founded UN began to draft a convention prohibiting the crime of genocide. The definition of this crime was controversial from the very beginning, with significant disagreements between States on its scope and nature. Genocide was affirmed as a crime under general international law by the General Assembly in Resolution 96(I) of 1946.[57] The contours of the crime were further developed in the Genocide Convention, adopted in 1948.[58] Three legal experts had been appointed by the UN Secretary General to help draft the Convention, one of whom was Lemkin, who 'devoted an important part of his advocating efforts to persuading his colleagues [de Vabres and Pella] to include a provision criminalizing cultural genocide.'[59] However, he did not succeed. Article II of the Genocide Convention defines genocide as any of the following acts committed with intent to destroy, in whole or in part, a national, ethnical, racial, or religious group, as such:

(a) Killing members of the group;
(b) Causing serious bodily or mental harm to members of the group;
(c) Deliberately inflicting on the group conditions of life calculated to bring about its physical destruction in whole or in part;
(d) Imposing measures intended to prevent births within the group;
(e) Forcibly transferring children of the group to another group.

Earlier versions of the Convention had included the concept of 'cultural genocide.' The earliest draft of the Convention referred to '[s]ystematic destruction of historical or religious monuments or their diversion to alien uses' and 'destruction or dispers[al] of documents and objects of historical, artistic, or religious value and of objects used in religious worship.'[60] An amended version included '[d]estroying ... libraries, museums, schools, historical monuments, places of worship and other cultural institutions and object of the group,' with the intent to destroy that group, as an act of

---

57 *The Crime of Genocide*, GA Res 96(I), UN GAOR, 1st sess, 55th mtg, UN Doc A/ES/96(I), (11 December 1946).
58 Convention on the Prevention and Punishment of the Crime of Genocide, opened for signature 9 December 1948, 78 UNTS 277.
59 Elise Novic, *The Concept of Cultural Genocide* (Oxford University Press 2016), 24.
60 Draft Convention on the Crime of Genocide, UN ESCOR, UN Doc E/447, 26 June 1947, pt 1, Article I(II)(3)(e).

genocide.⁶¹ While State representatives clearly decried the destruction of cultural heritage during the debates on the Convention, there was a feeling among many delegates that there was an obvious distinction between cultural genocide and physical and biological attacks on a group. Novic comments that '[f]rom the debates, one can acknowledge that it was not the concept of cultural genocide itself that was questioned, even if it might have been considered to be a somewhat "nebulous concept".'⁶² While delegates generally acknowledged that genocide could be committed in ways apart from physical or biological, it was felt that the time had not yet come for including such a view in a legal instrument. In this context, Schabas comments that

> [t]his was not really a rejection of [Lemkin's] thesis by which a group may be destroyed through attacks on its economy, its cultural bodies and its political institutions. Rather, it was simply a case of the world not being ready for such an innovative proposal in a binding treaty.⁶³

However, some States expressed the view that the acceptance of cultural genocide as part of the definition of genocide could interfere with their assimilation policies and undermine their concept of national unity.⁶⁴ The feeling of the majority of States was that such a concept would be better dealt with in an instrument on minority groups, and they looked to the drafting of the Universal Declaration of Human Rights (UDHR) as a more suitable process to address this issue.⁶⁵ The problem was, essentially, passed on to the General Assembly and its Third Committee, which was in charge of drafting the UDHR; however, the negotiations on the UDHR also failed to address the issue of minority rights in a significant way.⁶⁶ Thus, the post-war

---

61 Ad Hoc Committee on Genocide, 'Report of the Committee and Draft Convention Drawn up by the Committee,' UN ESCOR, UN Doc E/794 (24 May 1948), annex, Article III(2).
62 Elise Novic, *The Concept of Cultural Genocide* (Oxford University Press 2016), 28.
63 William Schabas, 'Preface' in Raphael Lemkin, *Axis Rule in Occupied Europe: Laws of Occupation, Analysis of Government, and Proposals for Redress* (end edn, first published 1944, Lawbook Exchange, Ltd 2008), xiii.
64 UN Doc. A/C.6?SR.63, General Assembly Sixth Committee, 63rd Meeting, Thursday 30 September 1948, Egyptian Delegate's Statement, p. 1293; Brazilian Delegate's Statement, p. 1292. See Elise Novic, *The Concept of Cultural Genocide* (Oxford University Press 2016), 29.
65 ECOSOC, 'Ad Hoc Committee on Genocide: Summary Record of the Third Meeting' UN Doc E/AC.35/SR.3 (13 April 1948). See Elise Novic, *The Concept of Cultural Genocide* (Oxford University Press 2016), 25–26.
66 ECOSOC 'Two Hundred and Eighteenth Meeting: Draft Convention on the Crime of Genocide' E/SR.218 (26 August 1948). It is interesting to note, however, that several States

52 Potential paradigms

negotiations in the UN on genocide resulted in disappointment for Lemkin, with his original conception of genocide being reduced to the narrow scope in the Genocide Convention, and with the rejection of a provision on the rights of minorities from the text of the UDHR 'which was considered as a human rights counterpart to the criminal provision of cultural genocide.'[67]

The exclusion of cultural genocide from the Genocide Convention put a halt to the development of this concept within the legal framework. However, interest in the concept re-emerged during the 1970s in the context of indigenous peoples, and again in the 1990s in respect of the damage to cultural heritage which took place during the Balkan Wars. As highlighted by Novic, '[i]n both contexts, the use of the "cultural genocide" rhetoric has contributed to the dismissal of claims of genocide through the requalification of the facts under different labels, which are often considered as euphemisms of genocide.'[68]

Despite suggestions that the concept of cultural genocide should be reintroduced into the legal framework, and that attacks on culture should constitute genocide, the definition of genocide adopted in the Genocide Convention has been reproduced in statutes of international criminal tribunals without amendment; for example, it was reproduced *verbatim* in Article 4(2) of the ICTY Statute and in Article 2(2) of the International Criminal Tribunal for Rwanda (ICTR) Statute. The basis for the reiteration of the language of the Genocide Convention in the ICTY Statute was justified as the UN Secretary General had declared that the Genocide Convention's definition was reflective of customary law.[69] The same definition was restated in Article 17 of the Draft Code of Crimes adopted by the International Law Commission in 1996. The Commentary to the Draft Code refers to the issue of cultural genocide, stating:

> As clearly shown by the preparatory work for the Convention, the destruction in question is the material destruction of a group either by

---

who had previously supported the insertion of a provision dealing with cultural genocide in the UDHR actually then opposed such an insertion of a provision dealing with minority rights in this instrument. See Elise Novic, *The Concept of Cultural Genocide* (Oxford University Press 2016), 30.

67 Elise Novic, *The Concept of Cultural Genocide* (Oxford University Press 2016), 17.
68 Ibid., 38.
69 Report of the Secretary General Pursuant to Para. 2 of Security Council Resolution 808 (1993), UN Doc S/25704, 12. In this report, the Secretary General made reference to the International Court of Justice (ICJ) Advisory Opinion in the *Reservations to the Convention on the Prevention and Punishment of the Crime of Genocide* [1951] ICJ Rep 15, 23.

physical or by biological means, not the destruction of the national, linguistic, religious, cultural or other identity of a particular group. The national or religious element and the racial or ethnic element are not taken into consideration in the definition of the word 'destruction', which must be taken only in its material sense, its physical or biological sense. It is true that the 1947 draft Convention prepared by the Secretary-General and the 1948 draft prepared by the *Ad Hoc* Committee on Genocide contained provisions on 'cultural genocide' covering any deliberate act committed with the intent to destroy the language, religion or culture of a group, such as prohibiting the use of the language of the group in daily intercourse or in schools or the printing and circulation of publications in the language of the group or destroying or preventing the use of libraries, museums, schools, historical monuments, places of worship or other cultural institutions and objects of the group. However, the text of the Convention, as prepared by the Sixth Committee and adopted by the General Assembly, did not include the concept of 'cultural genocide' contained in the two drafts and simply lists acts which come within the category of 'physical' or 'biological' genocide. The first three subparagraphs of the present article list acts of 'physical genocide,' while the last two list acts of 'biological genocide'.[70]

Article 6 of the Rome Statute of the ICC also reproduced the wording of the Genocide Convention,[71] and indeed, the issue of cultural genocide did not even come up for discussion when the ICC Statute was being drafted.

The concept of cultural genocide as a dimension of the crime of genocide has also been rejected in jurisprudence of international criminal tribunals. In the case of *Prosecutor v Kristić*, the Tribunal recalled the drafting of the Genocide Convention and the opinion of the International Law Commission and found that 'customary international law limits the definition of genocide to those acts seeking the physical or biological destruction of all or part of the group' with the result that

> an enterprise attacking only the cultural or sociobiological characteristics of a human group in order to annihilate these elements which give

---

70 Report of the International Law Commission on the Work of its Forty-Eighth Session, UN Doc A/51/10, 90–91.
71 Article 6, Statute of the International Criminal Court (1998), 2187 UNTS 90.

to that group its own identity distinct from the rest of the community would not fall under the definition of genocide.[72]

However, the Chamber added to this statement, commenting:

> The Trial Chamber however points out that where there is physical or biological destruction there are often simultaneous attacks on the cultural and religious property and symbols of the targeted group as well, attacks which may legitimately be considered as evidence of an intent to physically destroy the group. In this case, the Trial Chamber will thus take into account as evidence of intent to destroy the group the deliberate destruction of mosques and houses belonging to members of the group.[73]

This stance was confirmed as correct by the Appeals Chamber, which accepted that the definition of genocide in the Genocide Convention reflected customary law.[74]

The International Court of Justice (ICJ) also expressed a similar understanding concerning the scope of genocide in the *Application of the Genocide Convention* case, where it stated that

> [I]n the Court's view, the destruction of historical, cultural and religious heritage cannot be considered to constitute the deliberate infliction of conditions of life calculated to bring about the physical destruction of the group. Although such destruction may be highly significant inasmuch as it is directed to the elimination of all traces of the cultural or religious presence of a group, and contrary to other legal norms, it does not fall within the categories of acts of genocide set out in Article II of the Convention. In this regard, the Court observes that, during its consideration of the draft text of the Convention, the Sixth Committee of the General Assembly decided not to include cultural genocide in the list of punishable acts. Moreover, the ILC subsequently confirmed this approach ... Furthermore, the ICTY took a similar view in the *Kristić* case, finding that even in customary law, 'despite recent developments', the definition of acts of genocide is limited to those seeking the physical or biological destruction of a group. The Court concludes that the destruction of historical, religious and cultural heritage cannot

---

72 *Prosecutor v Kristić (Judgment)*, IT-98-33-T, 2 August 2001, para. 580.
73 Ibid.
74 *Prosecutor v Kristić (Judgment)*, IT-98-33-A, 19 April 2004, para. 25.

be considered to be a genocidal act within the meaning of Article II of the Genocide Convention.[75]

The Court added

> At the same time, [the Court] also endorses the observation made in the *Kristić* case that 'where there is physical or biological destruction there are often simultaneous attacks on the cultural and religious property and symbols of the targeted group as well, attacks which may legitimately be considered as evidence of an intent to physically destroy the group.'[76]

Cultural genocide and indigenous peoples

Novic comments that

> [t]wice in the story of contemporary international law has cultural genocide almost walked through its door. The first time was in 1948, when the draft provision on cultural genocide was finally rejected from the final definition of genocide … The second was in 2007, when a draft provision on cultural genocide and genocide was eventually substituted with another related to the 'elimination of cultures', during the negotiations of the United Nations Declaration on the Right of Indigenous Peoples (UNDRIP).[77]

The 2007 UNDRIP negotiations had been preceded by significant activism by, and on behalf of, indigenous peoples for many years, focusing on developing a framework of rights for indigenous peoples in addition to a recognition of the wrongs which had been done to them in the past. This included an acknowledgement of the destruction of their languages, their customs, and their culture as a result of colonisation and oppression. Luck comments that '[t]he increasing political activism of indigenous peoples in the 1970s and early 1980s provided a political opening for the return of cultural genocide to international discourse, though in a somewhat altered form.'[78] Novic opines

---

75 *Application of the Convention on the Prevention and Punishment of the Crime of Genocide (Bosnia and Herzegovina v Serbia and Montenegro) (Merits)* [2007] ICJ Rep 4, 124, para. 344.
76 Ibid.
77 Elise Novic, *The Concept of Cultural Genocide* (Oxford University Press 2016), 9–10.
78 Edward C Luck, 'Cultural Genocide and the Protection of Cultural Heritage,' J Paul Getty Trust Occasional Papers in Cultural Heritage Policy, Number 2 (2018), 26.

56 Potential paradigms

that it was in the context of developing UNDRIP and focusing on the experience of indigenous peoples that the idea of cultural genocide 'became progressively detached from the concept of genocide, to become an alternative form of genocide of its own: "ethnocide".'[79] Indeed, the word 'ethnocide' was included in Article 7 of the Draft Declaration on the Rights of Indigenous Peoples, which stated that 'indigenous peoples have the collective and individual right not to be subjected to ethnocide and cultural genocide' and called for the 'prevention of and redress for' a number of acts, starting with 'any action which has the aim or effect of depriving them of their integrity as distinct peoples, or of their cultural values or ethnic identities.'[80] The use of the terms 'cultural genocide' and 'ethnocide' was still very controversial, and States were very hesitant to accept the draft. Eventually, they were deleted, and the provision which was adopted, Article 7(2), states that

> indigenous peoples have the collective right to live in freedom, peace and security as distinct peoples and shall not be subjected to any act of genocide or any other act of violence, including forcibly removing children of the group to another group.[81]

The concept of cultural genocide of indigenous peoples was discussed in some depth in respect of the 'Stolen Generations' in Australia. Between 1910 and 1970, several various governmental policies facilitated the forcible removal of indigenous children from their families. The report of the National Inquiry into these removals, the 'Bringing them Home' report,[82] referred to the Genocide Convention[83] and described them as state-sponsored genocide.[84] However, the chairperson of the Inquiry later stated that '[w]ith hindsight, I think it was a mistake to use the word genocide ... once you latch onto the term "genocide", you're arguing about the intent and

---

79 Elise Novic, *The Concept of Cultural Genocide* (Oxford University Press 2016), 17.
80 UN Document, E/CN.4/Sub.2/1993/29. The Draft Declaration is included in Annex I of the Report of the Working Group on Indigenous Populations on its Eleventh Session, 23 August 1993, UN Commission on Human Rights, 45th Session, Agenda Item 15, 52.
81 Article 7(2), United Nations Declaration on the Rights of Indigenous Peoples, adopted by the General Assembly, 2 October 2007, A/RES/61/295.
82 Human Rights and Equal Opportunity Commission, *Report of the National Inquiry into the Separation of Aboriginal and Torres Strait Islander Children from their Families* (1997).
83 *Convention on the Prevention and Punishment of the Crime of Genocide*, opened for signature 9 December 1948, 1021 UNTS 78.
84 *Human Rights and Equal Opportunity Commission, Report of the National Inquiry into the Separation of Aboriginal and Torres Strait Islander Children from their Families* (1997), 270–275.

Potential paradigms 57

we should never have used it.'[85] Indeed, it is very difficult to prove that the *mens rea* of the crime of genocide, that is, the intent to destroy, in whole or in part, a national, ethnical, racial or religious group, was met in respect of the Stolen Generations, as all of the relevant legislation which permitted children to be taken away without the consent of parents was framed in terms of 'welfare.'

As pointed out by van Krieken, the Genocide Convention

> was really an unlikely ally for any attempt to deal with the harms inflicted by the removals of Aboriginal children from their families, having been produced by an organisation, the United Nations, that was broadly in support of the full assimilation of Indigenous peoples in a range of settler-colonial settings.[86]

Van Krieken asks if '[i]t is possible to have both a narrow, legally legitimate conception of genocide, but also a broader one that does justice to the violence at the heart of the settler-colonial project.'[87] He further comments that that

> [i]t ought to be possible to distinguish between, on the one hand, the understanding we rely on to attribute criminal responsibility and, on the other hand, the one we use to approach our history and our sense of what it means to be settler-colonial subjects.[88]

It is clear that while there is a desire to use the term genocide in respect of attacks on culture, an uneasiness remains with the concept of cultural genocide, and it still remains outside of the accepted legal framework.[89] Therefore, when assessing possible paradigms to deal with the protection of cultural heritage during armed conflict, it is doubtful whether engaging the cultural genocide framework would be beneficial. Indeed, Luck comments that

> [i]t would be more distorting than clarifying to view contemporary threats to cultural heritage solely through a cultural genocide lens. The

---

85 *The Bulletin* (Sydney), 12 June 2001, 27.
86 Robert van Krieken, 'Cultural Genocide Reconsidered' (2008) 12 *Australian Indigenous Law Review* 76, 76.
87 Ibid.
88 Ibid., 77.
89 Novic comments that the 'concept of cultural genocide ... was doomed to evolve outside the legal sphere. Elise Novic, *The Concept of Cultural Genocide* (Oxford University Press 2016), 17.

deficits are obvious. Cultural genocide lacks a clear or accepted definition. The notion of cultural genocide has never been defined, accepted, or codified by the world's governments. It was controversial when first raised in the 1940s and remains so today.[90]

Conclusion

The recent spate of attacks on cultural heritage has triggered significant analysis of its protective framework and resulted in various proposals for paradigms which would support and enhance this framework. Some of most noteworthy proposals focus on cultural cleansing, the R2P doctrine and cultural genocide. With regard to the former, while the use of the term was very useful in describing the extent and impact of attacks on cultural heritage on local communities and the world at large, this concept lacks a solid legal basis. It focused the world's attention on the cultural heritage crisis and highlighted the need for a new protective paradigm. While it cannot, of itself, be used as part of the legal framework, this label engendered discussions of other potential protective paradigms, including the R2P doctrine.

As highlighted in this chapter, the application of the R2P doctrine to the destruction of cultural heritage has found significant support in academia and in international organisations. However, while UNESCO has argued that the R2P doctrine can, and indeed, should, be applied to the protection of cultural heritage in armed conflict,[91] the organisation has yet to undertake significant analysis on the practical application of the doctrine to the protection of cultural heritage. Similarly, in academia, the theoretical application of the R2P doctrine to the destruction of cultural heritage has been supported, but numerous practical difficulties remain. It is, therefore, unlikely that, as it currently stands, the R2P doctrine would be an effective doctrine for the protection of cultural heritage.

Finally, the cultural genocide paradigm has also been proposed to further the protection of cultural heritage. While Lemkin's original conception of genocide would have included the destruction of heritage, and the revisiting of the concept decades after it was discarded from the text of the Genocide Convention illustrates a persistent which 'suggests that Lemkin was on to something when he sought to weave cultural, physical, and biological

---

90 Edward C Luck, 'Cultural Genocide and the Protection of Cultural Heritage,' J Paul Getty Trust Occasional Papers in Cultural Heritage Policy, Number 2 (2018), 27.
91 See UNESCO Expert Meeting on the 'Responsibility to Protect': Final Report (26–27 November 2015) http://www.unesco.org/new/en/culture/themes/armed-conflict-and-heritage/meetings-and-conferences/november-expert-meeting-responsibility-to-protect/ accessed 10 November 2019.

destruction into a larger pattern or strategy,'[92] given the stagnation of the definition of the crime in its 1948 formulation and the jurisprudence of international criminal tribunals on the issue of cultural genocide, it is also unfortunately doubtful if this would be a useful paradigm for the protection of cultural heritage.

However, the UN has developed another approach to the protection of cultural heritage, which is linked in ways to these paradigms. The use of the term cultural cleansing has encouraged the organisation to view the recent events in the Middle East and North Africa within a framework of peace and security. Thus, a security paradigm for the protection of cultural heritage is now developing, which is the focus of the next chapter.

---

92 Edward C Luck, 'Cultural Genocide and the Protection of Cultural Heritage,' J Paul Getty Trust Occasional Papers in Cultural Heritage Policy, Number 2 (2018), 28.

3 The securitisation of cultural heritage

Introduction

Even though a substantial legal framework seeking to protect cultural heritage during armed conflict exists, the recent attacks on cultural heritage in the Middle East and Africa illustrate that a different approach to the problem is required.[1] Recent attacks have also triggered a reassessment of the rationale for the protection of cultural heritage. Such a reassessment was seen when the United Nations (UN) facilitated a meeting on 21 September 2017 entitled 'Protecting Cultural Heritage from Terrorism and Mass Atrocities: Links and Common Responsibilities,' in which numerous international diplomats, non-governmental organisation (NGO) representatives, and experts participated. The event was hosted by the European Union Delegation to the UN, the Permanent Mission of Italy to the UN, the United Nations Educational, Scientific and Cultural Organization (UNESCO), the United Nations Office on Drugs and Crime, and the Global Centre for the Responsibility to Protect. Here, a security rationale for the protection of cultural heritage was highlighted. This approach moves on from the 'civilian use' and the 'culture-value' paradigms discussed in Chapter 1; builds on, to a certain extent, the 'cultural cleansing' paradigm discussed in Chapter 2; and focuses on the important role which culture plays in the maintenance of international peace and security and in the rebuilding of societies post-conflict. This meeting thus concluded in consensus that

> cultural heritage is worthy of protection, not only because it represents the rich and diverse legacy of human artistic and engineering ingenuity, but also because it is intertwined with the very survival of a people as

---

1 Edward C Luck, 'Cultural Genocide and the Protection of Cultural Heritage,' J Paul Getty Trust Occasional Papers in Cultural Heritage Policy, Number 2 (2018), 12.

a source of collective identity and the revitalization of civil society and economic vitality post-conflict.[2]

Furthermore, during the past few years, the Security Council has adopted a number of resolutions highlighting the link between cultural heritage and peace; for example, Resolution 2347 recognises that

> the looting of cultural property in the event of armed conflicts ... and the attempt to deny historical roots and cultural diversity in this context can fuel and exacerbate conflict and hamper post-conflict national reconciliation, thereby undermining the security, stability, governance, social, economic and cultural development of affected States.[3]

Thus, it can be said that, cultural heritage has, recently, become securitised. It is important to note, however, that the relationship between cultural heritage and peace and security is not a new one. At the Conference for the Establishment of UNESCO, the New Zealand delegate, Arnold Campbell, made a linkage between peace, democracy, and education, which became the main aim of the new organisation, that is, to contribute to peace and security throughout the world by 'promoting collaboration among nations through education, science, culture and communication in order to further universal respect for justice, the rule of law, human rights and fundamental freedoms set out in the Charter of the United Nations.'[4] However, this relationship is now being re-emphasised and made explicit by the UN. The securitisation of cultural heritage has now come to the fore in global discourse and is a central component of the current global response to its destruction during armed conflict. This leaning towards a security paradigm on the protection of cultural heritage is evident in the development of 'cultural peacekeeping' and in the growing importance apportioned to culture and cultural heritage in peacebuilding initiatives.

Reviewing the various traditional approaches to protecting cultural heritage, Luck comments that 'for those seeking a more robust international response to attacks on cultural heritage, there is a strong inclination to label

---

2 Thomas G Weiss and Nina Connolly, 'Cultural Cleansing and Mass Atrocities,' J Paul Getty Occasional Paper in Cultural Heritage Policy, Number 1 (2017), 4.
3 Preamble, UN SC Res 2347 (24 March 2017).
4 Janet Blake, *International Cultural Heritage Law*, (Oxford University Press 2015), xv. See V Pavone, 'From the Labyrinth of the World to the Paradise of the Heart: Science and Humanism' (Lexington Books 2008), 1.

such assaults as a matter of international peace and security.'[5] This approach is understandable within the context of the UN, given that threats to international peace and security can trigger the Security Council's enforcement framework and focus the attention of the UN Permanent Five on such destruction. Luck is of the opinion that when Irina Bokova, the then Director General of UNESCO, began to employ the term cultural cleansing in 2014 and 2015, 'she put it squarely in a security context.'[6] Therefore, as highlighted in Chapter 2, while the term itself is ambiguous, without an explicit accompanying legal framework, its use has succeeded in garnering the attention of the Security Council and has forestalled the securitisation of cultural heritage. The Copenhagen School has developed the securitisation model, which posits that any subject can become a matter of 'security', changing it from a state of non-politicisation to one of politicisation, whereby it becomes an aspect of public policy, which requires state attention and action; and finally to a state of securitisation, where it becomes a matter of priority which must be urgently addressed.[7] Clearly, the destruction of cultural heritage must be a priority for the international community given recent attacks and the significant damage caused to the identity and future of minority groups.

This is an important move in the context of cultural heritage, with securitisation engendering the establishment of concrete measures, within the UN framework, aimed at the protection of cultural heritage, including the deployment of peacekeeping missions with a cultural heritage protection mandate. Foradori and Rosa state that this new 'cultural peacekeeping'

> has emerged primarily as the outcome of a process of 'securitization' of cultural heritage destruction ... ISIS' iconoclasm has been rendered a security threat thereby allowing the international community to resort to strong and extraordinary measures – beyond the realm of standard political norms and procedures – to address this recently emerged threat.[8]

---

5 Edward C Luck, 'Cultural Genocide and the Protection of Cultural Heritage,' J Paul Getty Trust Occasional Papers in Cultural Heritage Policy, Number 2 (2018), 13.
6 Ibid.
7 See Ole Waever, 'Securitisation and Desecuritisation,' in Ronnie D Lischutz (ed), *On Security* (Columbia University Press 1995), 46. See also Barry Buzan, Ole Waever, and Japp de Wilde, *Security: A New Framework for Analysis* (Lynne Rienner 1998).
8 Paolo Foradori and Paolo Rosa, 'Expanding the Peacekeeping Agenda. The Protection of Cultural Heritage in War-Torn Societies' (2017) 29(2) *Global Change, Peace and Security* 145, 151.

This chapter seeks to analyse the securitisation of cultural heritage and investigate how framing the destruction of cultural heritage as a peace and security issue within the UN structure can help to better protect it. Luck states that '[a] security lens can bring substantive, conceptual, and political benefits to the consideration of ways to counter the destruction of the world's cultural heritage.'[9] This chapter thus analyses the benefits of this approach. The first section discusses a number of UN resolutions which have addressed the protection of cultural heritage within a security framework. The second section focuses on the topic of cultural peacekeeping, while the third addresses the role of cultural heritage in peacebuilding.

UN resolutions on cultural heritage

The UN Security Council has been a lawmaker in the field of cultural heritage. In the past, the Council generally referred to cultural heritage in specific armed conflicts in its resolutions; for example, in 1999, the Council adopted a resolution on Afghanistan and called for 'respect for Afghanistan's cultural and historical heritage.'[10] In respect of the conflict in Iraq in 2003, the Council underlined 'the need for respect for the archaeological, historical, cultural, and religious heritage of Iraq, and for the continued protection of archaeological, historical, cultural, and religious sites, museums, libraries, and monuments.'[11] Similarly, in 2012, it highlighted the need for the protection of cultural heritage in Mali, and strongly condemned 'the desecration, damage and destruction of sites of holy, historic and cultural significance, especially but not exclusively those designated UNESCO World Heritage sites, including in the city of Timbuktu.'[12] The Council also adopted a number of resolutions with regard to Syria and included wording on the protection of cultural heritage therein. For example, in Resolution 2139, the Council called on the parties to 'save Syria's rich societal mosaic and cultural heritage and take appropriate steps to ensure the protection of Syria's World Heritage Sites.'[13]

The Council has adopted a number of resolutions which supplement and reinforce the extant legal framework on international cultural heritage

---

9 Edward C Luck, 'Cultural Genocide and the Protection of Cultural Heritage,' J Paul Getty Trust Occasional Papers in Cultural Heritage Policy, Number 2 (2018), 13.
10 UN SC Res 1267 (15 October 1999) UN Doc S/RES/1267, Preamble.
11 UN SC Res 1483 (22 May 2003) UN Doc S/RES/1483, para 7.
12 UN SC Res 2056 (5 July 2012) UN Doc S/RES/2056. The Security Council adopted a number of other resolutions in respect of Mali – see UNSC Res 2085 (20 December 2012) UN Doc S/RES/2085, and UN SC Res 2100 (25 April 2013) UN Doc S/RES/2100.
13 UN SC Res 2139 (22 February 2014) UN Doc S/RES/2139.

obligations. For example, Resolution 1483 (2003) underlined the binding obligation on the international community to counteract the crimes against cultural heritage committed in armed conflicts, and stated that all Member States were bound

> to take appropriate steps to facilitate the safe return to Iraqi institutions of Iraqi cultural property and other items of archaeological, historical, cultural, rare scientific, and religious importance illegally removed from the Iraq National Museum, the National Library, and other locations in Iraq.[14]

It thus emphasised an *erga omnes* obligation to ensure that cultural property illegally transferred from occupied territories would be returned.

Other resolutions have highlighted the link between looting of cultural artefacts and the financing of terrorism. The first Security Council resolution which linked cultural heritage and terrorism was Resolution 1267, adopted in 1999, with regard to the Taliban and the heritage of Afghanistan.[15] In Resolution 2199 (2015), the Council underlined the link between trafficking in cultural artefacts and the financing of terrorism, noting that

> terrorist groups are generating income from engaging directly or indirectly in the looting and smuggling of cultural heritage items from archaeological sites, museums, libraries, archives, and other sites in Iraq and Syria, which is being used to support their recruitment efforts and strengthen their operational capability to organize and carry out terrorist attacks.[16]

This resolution also called on Member States to take action to prevent trade in cultural property from Iraq and Syria and called for co-operation between UNESCO, Interpol and other organisations to support this effort.[17] This has resulted in the strengthening of domestic law on trafficking, in addition to co-operation between States and organisations on this issue.[18]

It is thus clear that the Security Council has adopted a multidimensional approach to the protection of cultural heritage by, for example, including the prohibition of the use of funds to directly or indirectly benefit ISIS;

---

14 UN SC Res 1483 (22 May 2003) UN Doc S/RES/1483, para. 7.
15 UN SC Res 1267 (1999).
16 UN SC Res 2199 (12 February 2015) UN Doc S/RES/2199, paras. 15–16.
17 Ibid., para. 717.
18 Intervention of Ms Bokova at the Security Council briefing meeting, UN Doc S/PV.7909 (24 March 2017) 4.

demanding that all UN Member States take appropriate measures to prevent trade in Iraqi and Syrian cultural heritage; calling on international organisations, such as Interpol and UNESCO, to assist with the efforts to counter extremism and intolerance within Iraq and Syria through education and strengthening of civil society.[19]

The destruction of cultural heritage as a peace and security issue in UN resolutions

Recent Security Council resolutions have reflected the securitisation trend in respect of cultural heritage, with the Council explicitly linking the destruction of cultural property with the maintenance of international peace and security. For example, Resolution 2199 (2015), adopted under Chapter VII of the UN Charter, condemned 'the destruction of cultural heritage in Iraq and Syria ... whether such destruction is incidental or deliberate, including targeted destruction of religious sites and objects', and identified attacks by groups such as ISIL as a threat to international peace and security.[20] This approach was also followed in Resolution 2249 (2015), where the Security Council affirmed that

> by its violent extremist ideology, its terrorist acts, its continued gross systematic and widespread attacks directed against civilians, abuses of human rights and violations of international humanitarian law, including those driven on religious or ethnic ground, its eradication of cultural heritage and trafficking of cultural property ... the Islamic State in Iraq and the Levant (ISIL, also known as Da'esh), constitutes a global and unprecedented threat to international peace and security.

The securitisation trend in these resolutions was significantly heightened in Resolution 2347, adopted in 2017.

UN Security Council Resolution 2347 (2017)

On 24 March 2017, in the midst of the recent, highly devastating spate of targeted attacks on cultural heritage in the Middle East, the Security Council adopted Resolution 2347.[21] Its importance has been highlighted in a number

---

19 See James Cuno, 'The Responsibility to Protect the World's Cultural Heritage' (2016) 23 *Brown J World Affairs* 97, 101.
20 UN SC Res 2199 (12 February 2015) UN Doc S/RES/2199, para. 15.
21 'Maintenance of International Peace and Security' (24 March 2017) UN Doc S/RES/2347.

of sources, and it has been described as a milestone in the global response to the destruction of cultural heritage.[22] The resolution is noteworthy because it is the first Security Council resolution which is focused *solely* on the destruction and trafficking of cultural heritage in the context of armed conflict.[23] Thus, while it is not the first resolution to address the destruction and looting of cultural heritage, 'by dedicating an entire resolution on this topic it affirms the protection of cultural heritage as a key means for the maintenance of international peace and security.'[24] Haulser comments that this is

> significant as it means that attacks against cultural heritage are now considered on a similar level as other threats to international peace, which have also been addressed with specific resolutions, such as the proliferation of weapons of mass destruction or arms trafficking.[25]

The acceptance of the destruction of cultural heritage as a threat to international peace was highlighted during the Security Council Briefing on Resolution 2347, convened under a British presidency by Ambassador Peter Wilson, who noted the requirement to react to the destruction of cultural heritage 'with the same intensity and the same unity of purpose as any other threat to international peace and security.'[26] At the adoption of Resolution 2347, the UN Under-Secretary General for Political Affairs commented that the protection of cultural heritage 'is not only a cultural issue, it is also a security and humanitarian imperative.'[27] He further stated that terrorist groups do not only 'exploit cultural site[s] to finance their activities' but also 'destroy and traffic cultural heritage to undermine the power of culture

---

22 See A Azoulay, 'Historic Milestone for the Protection of Cultural Heritage' (24 March 2017) https://onu.delegfrance.org/Historic-milestone-for-the-protection-of-cultural-heritage accessed 10 November 2019. I Bokova, 'United Nations Security Council Resolution 2347' (24 March 2017) UNESCO Doc. CL/4210. See also Andrzej Jakubowski, 'Resolution 2347: Mainstreaming the Protection of Cultural Heritage at the Global Level' (2018) 48 *Questions of International Law* 21.
23 See Andrzej Jakubowski, 'Resolution 2347: Mainstreaming the Protection of Cultural Heritage at the Global Level' (2018) 48 *Questions of International Law* 21, 21.
24 Kristin Hausler, 'Cultural Heritage and the Security Council: Why Resolution 2347 Matters' (2018) 48 *Question of International Law* 5, 12.
25 Ibid., 5.
26 Foreign and Commonwealth Office and Peter Wilson CMG, UK Mission to the United Nations, New York, Statement by Ambassador Peter Wilson, UK Deputy Permanent Representative to the United Nations, at the Security Council briefing on Protecting Cultural Heritage (24 March 2017), www.gov.uk/government/speeches/what-were-witnessing-is-a-systematic-and-corrosive-assault-on-history-on-religion-on-the-very-fabric-of-identity accessed 10 November 2019.
27 Intervention of Mr Feltman, UN Doc S/PV.7907 (24 March 2017) 2–3.

as a bridge between generations and people of different backgrounds and religions.'[28] In addition, he commented that Resolution 2347 was not only focused on depriving 'terrorists of funding, but also to protect cultural heritage as a symbol of understanding and respect for all religions, beliefs and civilisations.' [29]

The resolution acknowledges the many and varied aspects of cultural heritage and the consequent all-pervasive impact of its destruction on the local and global community. It highlights the multifaceted nature of cultural heritage protection and notes various issues which must be addressed in order to enhance this protection. Jakubowski comments that the resolution 'constitutes the first global initiative by the UNSC integrating and consolidating various elements of international law and policy vis-à-vis cultural heritage.'[30] Further underlining the significance of this resolution, he states that its

> significance ... goes far beyond the enhancement of obligations imposed on all the UN members to prosecute and punish cultural heritage crimes. In fact, it may be argued that the UNSC has opted for mainstreaming of the protection of cultural heritage in armed conflicts within a broader global agenda.[31]

This resolution will thus, hopefully, initiate an improved, multilayered protective framework for cultural heritage during armed conflict, acknowledging, as it does, the role that such heritage plays in the maintenance of international peace and security. While it has been vaunted as a seminal development in the protection of cultural heritage and is indeed a significant development in cultural heritage protection, the resolution nevertheless includes a number of weak points, to be discussed here.

The Preamble of the resolution underscores that

> unlawful destruction of cultural heritage, and the looting and smuggling of cultural property in the event of armed conflicts ... , and the attempt to deny historical roots and cultural diversity in this context can fuel and exacerbate conflict and hamper post-conflict national

---

28 Ibid.
29 Ibid.
30 Andrzej Jakubowski, 'Resolution 2347: Mainstreaming the Protection of Cultural Heritage at the Global Level' (2018) 48 *Questions of International Law* 21, 21.
31 Ibid., 34.

reconciliation, thereby undermining the security, stability, governance, social, economic and cultural development of affected States.[32]

It is clear from this phrasing that the Security Council acknowledges the 'culture-value' approach to the protection of cultural heritage, and that it, in addition, acknowledges its protection as a security imperative. The resolution also firmly links the plunder of cultural goods and their consequent illicit trafficking with the financial fuelling of armed conflict, which impacts on international peace and security.[33] Thus, the international discourse on cultural heritage is now centrally located within a peace and security framework.

The resolution underlines the importance of inter-State co-operation, in addition to co-operation between States and organisations in addressing the challenges of the destruction of cultural heritage. It therefore calls for enhanced co-operation between States and non-State actors operating on both the international and national fora at varying levels, including UNESCO, the World Customs Organization, Interpol, and the UN Office on Drugs and Crime. Alongside enhanced collaboration among international organisations and agencies, the resolution also states that the Security Council promotes the participation of civic society, including experts and practitioners, in elaborating 'standards of provenance documentation, differentiated due diligence and all measures to prevent the trade of stolen or illegally trade cultural property.'[34] The promotion of enhanced international collaboration and co-operation in the field of cultural heritage, and the broadening of its scope to include not just inter-State co-operation but also collaboration between organisations, agencies, and other stakeholders such as non-State actors, is significant and praiseworthy because

> [s]uch a conceptualization and eventual implementation of global objectives and solidarity in the realm of cultural heritage protection will arguably contribute to more effective global governance in times of crisis.[35]

Resolution 2347 builds on the Abu Dhabi Declaration on Safeguarding Endangered Cultural Heritage 2016,[36] which foresaw the foundation of

---

32 UN SC Resolution 2347 (24 March 2017), Preamble, 5th recital.
33 Ibid., Preamble, 7th–10th recitals.
34 Ibid., para. 17(g).
35 Andrzej Jakubowski, 'Resolution 2347: Mainstreaming the Protection of Cultural heritage at the Global Level' (2018) 48 *Questions of International Law* 21–44, 43.
36 Conference on Safeguarding Endangered Cultural Heritage – Abu Dhabi Declaration (3 December 2016) www.diplomatie.gouv.fr/en/french-foreign-policy/cultural-diplomacy/eve

a fund dedicated to the protection of cultural heritage in armed conflict, in addition to the creation of a network of safe havens in respect of cultural heritage. While the fund idea is to be applauded, as financial help is most definitely needed to support the protection of cultural heritage, the resolution only encourages, rather than requires, UN member States 'to provide financial contributions to support preventive and emergency operations, fight the illicit trafficking of cultural property, as well as undertake all appropriate efforts for the recovery of cultural heritage, in the spirit of the principles of the UNESCO Conventions',[37] thus leaving a lot up to the political considerations of States. The safe havens envisaged in Resolution 2347 are to be established by States in their territories to protect cultural heritage while taking into account the 'cultural, geographic, and historic specificities of the cultural heritage in need of protection.'[38] While the idea of extraterritorial safe havens is not explicitly referred to in the resolution, the Security Council does not dismiss such a move.[39]

Jakubowski highlights the important contribution which Resolution 2347 has made to the protection of cultural heritage by taking an all-encompassing and multiforum approach to its protection, pointing out that it recognises and builds on different policy tools, including UNESCO's #Unite4Heritage campaign and the 2016 Abu Dhabi Declaration, in addition to technical tools created to address the illicit trafficking in cultural property, including the United Nations Office on Drugs and Crime (UNODC) SHERLOC online portal and the World Customs Organization (WCO) ARCHEO platform. He comments that

> [i]n this regard the UNSC has implicitly substantiated the idea of global cultural heritage governance built on a variety of institutions, mechanisms, relationships, and tools through which the collective interests of the international community in safeguarding cultural heritage in armed conflict are enhanced and implemented on the global plane.[40]

The main boon of the resolution, however, is in placing the issue of the destruction of cultural heritage during armed conflict squarely within the peace and security framework, and, in so doing, attracting the attention of

---

nts/article/conference-on-safeguarding-endangered-cultural-heritage-abu-dhabi-declaration accessed 10 November 2019.
37 UN SC Resolution 2347 (24 March 2017), para. 15.
38 Ibid., para. 16.
39 Andrzej Jakubowski, 'Resolution 2347: Mainstreaming the Protection of Cultural Heritage at the Global Level' (2018) 48 *Questions of International Law* 21, 37.
40 Ibid., 39.

the global community to the plight of cultural heritage and the significant impact of its loss on communities and the world at large. In developing the securitisation of cultural heritage paradigm, the resolution has

> integrated the often dispersed and fragmented regimes of international law – cultural heritage law, humanitarian law, criminal law, and State responsibility – with global, regional and national policies aimed at counteracting cultural heritage crimes committed in armed conflicts.[41]

Success of Resolution 2347

Has Resolution 2347 been successful in the protection of cultural heritage during armed conflict? This is a difficult question to answer definitively, but it is clear that the resolution has been taken seriously by States, as is evidenced by both political commitments in respect of the protection of cultural heritage as well as in the adoption of domestic legislation in line with the resolution. For example, the objectives of Resolution 2347 have been confirmed as political commitments by the G7 States,[42] and the 2017 Florence Declaration reaffirmed the importance of cultural heritage for human existence, global peace, and economic development.[43]

A number of States and intergovernmental organisations have submitted reports with respect to the implementation of the Resolution.[44] Some developments are noteworthy, including the creation of specialised units of heritage personnel within police forces and customs authorities, the provision of cultural heritage training to police, and improved databases for information collection, as well as enhanced international co-operation in the field of cultural heritage protection and the trafficking of cultural artefacts.[45]

There has been important collaboration and co-operation between organisations in the cultural heritage field following on from the Resolution. For example, in 2016, UNESCO and the International Committee of the Red

---

41 Ibid., 43.
42 The G7, originally G8, was set up in 1975 as an informal forum of the leaders of the world's leading industrial States. These are Canada, France, Germany, Italy, Japan, the United Kingdom, and the United States, with the European Union as an invitee.
43 Joint Declaration of the Ministers of Culture of G7 on the Occasion of the Meeting 'Culture as an Instrument for Dialogue among Peoples' (30–31 March 2017). The text of the Declaration is available at http://www.beniculturali.it/mibac/multimedia/MiBAC/documents/1490881204940_DECLARATION-Dichiarazione.pdf accessed 10 November.
44 Report of the Secretary-General on the implementation of Security Council Resolution 2347 (2017) UN Doc S/2017/969 (17 November 2017).
45 Ibid., 49–71.

Cross adopted a memorandum of understanding aimed at the integration of the protection of cultural heritage in humanitarian operations.[46] In addition, in November 2017, on the occasion of the 39th Session of UNESCO's General Conference, the then Director General of UNESCO, Irina Bokova, and the prosecutor of the International Criminal Court, Fatou Bensouda, signed a letter of intent in respect of collaboration and co-operation in the future on cultural heritage issues, through, for example, the provision of cultural expertise by UNESCO to the Court.[47] Relatedly, the Office of the Prosecutor has noted that during its Strategic Plan 2019–2021 it 'will finalise its ongoing work toward the adoption of a comprehensive policy on the protection of cultural heritage within the Rome Statute legal framework, which will also cover the important issue of victimisation in the context of such crimes.'[48]

In 2017, the Council of Europe adopted the Convention on Offences relating to Cultural Property, which references Resolution 2347 and focuses on the criminalisation of illicit trafficking in cultural objects, requiring States parties to criminalise intentional destruction of cultural property whether or not it has taken place in the context of an armed conflict.[49] This Convention thus extends the regime of the 1954 Hague Convention and its Second Protocol.

While there is much to be celebrated in Resolution 2347 in respect of furthering the protection of cultural heritage, it does contain a number of shortcomings. One of these is the dearth of discussion of intangible cultural heritage. In a previous resolution, Resolution 2170 (2014), the Security Council called on States to prevent the subversion of cultural institutions by terrorists and their supporters, thus implicitly expressing concern for intangible cultural heritage.[50] However, Resolution 2347 focuses primarily on tangible cultural heritage, deploring the 'destruction of religious sites and artefacts, as well as the looting and smuggling of cultural property from archaeological sites, museums, libraries, archives and other sites.'[51] While

---

46 Memorandum of Understanding between the United Nations Educational, Scientific and Cultural Organization and the ICRC (2016) available at https://unesdoc.unesco.org/ark:/48223/pf0000244256 accessed 10 November.
47 UNESCO, 'International Criminal Court and UNESCO Strengthen Co-operation on the Protection of Cultural Heritage' (6 November 2017) http://whc.unesco.org/en/news/1742 accessed 10 November 2019.
48 ICC Office of the Prosecutor, *Strategic Plan 2019–2021* (17 July 2019) available at https://www.icc-cpi.int/itemsDocuments/20190726-strategic-plan-eng.pdf accessed 10 November 2019, 5.
49 Council of Europe Treaty Series No 221, also known as the Nikosia Convention.
50 UN SC Resolution 2170 (15 August 2014) UN Doc S/RES/2170.
51 UN SC Resolution 2347 (24 March 2017) UN Doc S/RES/2347 para 1.

the Hague Convention 1954 and the Additional Protocols to the Geneva Conventions focus exclusively on tangible cultural heritage, the UNESCO Declaration concerning the Intentional Destruction of Cultural Heritage 2003 'addresses intentional destruction of cultural heritage including cultural heritage linked to a natural site.'[52] With regard to the current phenomenon of cultural heritage destruction, the UN Special Rapporteur in the field of cultural rights delved further into the issue of destruction of tangible and intangible cultural heritage and commented that an attack on one is often associated with an attack on the other.[53] Resolution 2347 makes an implicit reference to intangible cultural heritage, noting that the destruction of cultural heritage equates to an attempt to deny historical roots and cultural diversity. In addition, it also states that the destruction and looting of cultural heritage may undermine not only peace and security but also the 'social, economic and cultural development of affected States.'[54] However, intangible cultural heritage could have been the focus of greater attention. Further resolutions should fully embrace all forms of cultural heritage in order to ensure the greatest level of protection for culture and cultural diversity globally.

Also noteworthy is that while Resolution 2347 recognised the destruction of cultural heritage as a peace and security issue, the resolution was not adopted under Chapter VII of the UN Charter. The fact that the resolution was adopted outside of the Chapter VII framework may be 'worrisome,'[55] but it does not mean that the UN is powerless to deal with destruction of cultural heritage, as peacekeeping also falls outside this framework. Indeed, the recognition of the destruction of cultural heritage as a peace and security issue has opened up a discussion on the protection of cultural heritage within the peacekeeping realm, and 'cultural peacekeeping' and 'Blue Helmets for Culture' have now become a reality.

Cultural Peacekeeping

Peacekeepers have a duty to protect cultural heritage. This duty includes the obligation not to harm cultural heritage personally, but it also expands

---

52 Section II(1) UNESCO Declaration concerning the Intentional Destruction of Cultural Heritage (17 October 2003).
53 Report prepared by the Special Rapporteur in the field of cultural rights, Karima Bennoune, submitted in accordance with Human Rights Council Resolution 28/9 (9 August 2016) para. 6.
54 UN SC Resolution 2347 (24 March 2917) UN Doc S/RES/2347 Preamble.
55 Edward C Luck, 'Cultural Genocide and the Protection of Cultural Heritage,' J Paul Getty Trust Occasional Papers in Cultural Heritage Policy, Number 2 (2018), 14.

to encompass the obligation to prevent its damage, destruction, or misappropriation. Thus, Petrovic comments that '[a]ccordingly, the protection of precious cultural property should be part of the mandate of every peacekeeping mission.'[56] However, on reviewing peacekeeping mandates, and indeed, practice, over time, it is clear that the protection of cultural heritage has not been recognised as a priority, nor indeed has the wider concept of culture been recognised as an important element of peacekeeping missions.[57] This is an unfortunate omission, given that culture can be the reason behind a conflict, and indeed, as has been discussed in this book, can be the target of conflict.

With UN Security Council Resolution 2100 (2013), the protection of cultural heritage sites was included for the first time in the mandate of a UN Peacekeeping mission, the UN Multidimensional Integrated Stabilization Mission in Mali (MINUSMA). This resolution mandated MINUSMA 'to assist the transitional authorities of Mali, as necessary and feasible, in protecting from attack the cultural and historical sites in Mali, in collaboration with UNESCO.'[58] This resolution is significant, as it signals that the UN recognises the role of culture in peace resolution and post-conflict peacebuilding, and acknowledges that culture is inseparable from humanity. Following on from this resolution, MINUSMA has co-operated with various actors relevant to the protection of cultural heritage in Mali, including UNESCO and the Malian government, as well as affected communities. It has provided logistical support for the restoration of the mausoleums and some of the libraries that were destroyed or damaged in the attacks by Ansar Dine. In addition, and very significantly in terms of peacebuilding, it has aided the Malian government to create an inventory of intangible cultural heritage. MINMUSA's Environment and Culture Unit has also organised training aimed at understanding the importance of the preservation of Malian cultural heritage for participants in the mission.

It should be noted that the protection of cultural heritage is just one aspect of MINUSMA's mandate. Other tasks include the protection of civilians; the monitoring of human rights; the disarmament, demobilisation, and reintegration of armed forces; and providing support for elections, in addition to activities in the field of reconciliation and justice. This seemingly vast set of responsibilities 'has left many wondering how could MINUSMA stretch so widely to encompass the protection of cultural heritage in its

---

56 Jadranka Petrovic, 'The Cultural Dimension of Peace Operations: Peacekeeping and Cultural Property' in Andrew H Campbell (ed), *Global Leadership Initiatives in Conflict Resolution and Peacebuilding* (IGO Global 2018), 84, 95.
57 See ibid., 95, which states: 'At the practical level, culture, together with cultural property, has not been traditionally considered a priority in the context of peacekeeping.'
58 UN SC Resolution 2100 (25 April 2013).

mandate given it is generally not within the purview of peace operations.'[59] This query is answered somewhat by the Chief of the UN Department of Peace Operation's Policy and Best Practice Service, Leanne Smith, who comments that the inclusion of the phrase 'as necessary and feasible' in paragraph 16(f) of Resolution 2100 (2013) in relation to the extent to which the protection of cultural heritage falls within MINUSMA's mandate limits its scope somewhat, and illustrates that the protection of cultural heritage is not the Mission's primary concern. However, some commentators are nevertheless still critical of the Mission having such a broad mandate. For example, Karlsrud states that

> MINUSMA faces a very complicated situation on the ground, including the National Movement for the Liberation of Azawad (MNLA), which is fighting for autonomy for the North, the jihadists in AQIM, the Movement for Unity and Jihad in West Africa (MUJAO) and Ansar Eddine. In addition, various parts of the Government are involved in drug smuggling, which may involve some of the armed groups.[60]

Some might question the inclusion of the protection of cultural heritage in a peacekeeping mission's mandate, given that they have so many other priorities, including the protection of human life. However, its inclusion echoes the trend of securitisation of cultural heritage, with its protection being recognised as a threat to international peace and security. This move also follows on from the ICC's case of *Prosecutor v Al Mahdi*,[61] previously discussed, which involved the prosecution of an individual for crimes against cultural property, even when there was no loss of human life.

The mandate of MINUSMA was extended via Resolution 2295 (2016) until 30 June 2017,[62] and subsequently, to 30 June 2020.[63] In Resolution 2295, the Security Council clarified the role of the protection of cultural heritage in MINUSMA's mandate, and underlined that cultural protection is not among the mission mandate's 'priority' tasks.[64] However, paragraph

---

59 Jadranka Petrovic, 'The Cultural Dimension of Peace Operations: Peacekeeping and Cultural Property' in Andrew H Campbell (ed), *Global Leadership Initiatives in Conflict Resolution and Peacebuilding* (IGO Global 2018), 84, 98.
60 J Karlsrud, 'The UN at War: Examining the Consequences of Peace-Enforcement Mandates for the UN Peacekeeping Operations in the CAR, the DRC and Mali' (2015) 36(1) *Third World Quarterly* 40, 46.
61 *Prosecutor v Al Mahdi* ICC-01/12-01/15.
62 UN SC Resolution 2295 (29 June 2016).
63 UN SC Resolution 2480 (28 June 2019).
64 UN SC Resolution 2295 (29 June 2016), para. 19.

20(c) of the Resolution authorises MINUSMA to employ its existing capacities to aid in implementing certain tasks, including support for cultural preservation '[t]o assist the Malian authorities, as necessary and feasible, in protecting from attack the cultural and historical sites in Mali, in collaboration with UNESCO.'[65]

While it is significant that the protection of culture and cultural heritage has been included within the mandate of UN peacekeeping missions, it is important to note that the impact of this role has been limited by the Security Council. In Resolution 2347 (2017), the Council affirmed that UN peacekeeping operations can be involved in the protection of cultural heritage only 'when specifically mandated by the Security Council.'[66] This reflects the UN approach to questions of sovereignty, and highlights that States have the primary responsibility to protect cultural heritage within their borders. The Resolution underlines that the Security Council is unwilling to authorise an intervention in a State for the sole purpose of protecting cultural heritage in that State, or to extend the mandate of a peacekeeping mission to protect cultural heritage without the acquiescence of that State.[67] This stance is important with regard to the likelihood of the use of use of the R2P doctrine in respect of the protection of cultural heritage as discussed in Chapter 2.

Given that the protection of cultural heritage has been brought within the peace and security framework, it is to be expected that future peacekeeping missions will also have a cultural heritage protection mandate. Cultural peacekeeping can contribute to the protection of cultural heritage from damage and destruction by aiding in the enforcement of the international protection regime, including the implementation of the 1954 Hague Convention. In addition, cultural peacekeeping can support more conventional cultural protection approaches, including the UNESSCO–EU's Emergency Safeguarding of the Syrian Heritage Project, and the International Council of Museums Emergency Red List of Syrian Cultural Objects at Risk.[68] However,

---

65 Ibid., para. 20(c). See Jadranka Petrovic, 'The Cultural Dimension of Peace Operations: Peacekeeping and Cultural Property' in Andrew H Campbell (ed), *Global Leadership Initiatives in Conflict Resolution and Peacebuilding* (IGO Global 2018), 84, 99.
66 UN SC Resolution 2347 (24 March 2017).
67 See Jadranka Petrovic, 'The Cultural Dimension of Peace Operations: Peacekeeping and Cultural Property' in Andrew H Campbell (ed), *Global Leadership Initiatives in Conflict Resolution and Peacebuilding* (IGO Global 2018), 84, 100.
68 Paolo Foradori and Paolo Rosa, 'Expanding the Peacekeeping Agenda. The Protection of Cultural Heritage in War-Torn Societies' (2017) 29(2) *Global Change, Peace & Security* 145, 153.

> [t]he successful integration of the cultural perspective into a peace operation is ultimately dependent on the extent of education, training, understanding, tolerance, cooperation, and coordination between many diverse elements of any mission and, at the same time, and importantly, between the mission and the local population.[69]

Thus, in order for the paradigm of cultural peacekeeping to be effective, significant attention must be focused on the design and mandate of such missions, as well as how they will be perceived and received in the communities which they seek to protect.

An argument in favour of including the protection of cultural heritage within the scope of peacekeeping mandates, according to Witkam, is that 'protecting local heritage will help create goodwill with the local community'[70] and win hearts and minds at the local level. This can contribute to the successful achievement of the Mission's broader mandate. Petrovic comments that

> cultural property-inclusive peacekeeping ... is more likely to garner local support than a peacekeeping mission which does not incorporate cultural property in its mandate. Cultural property–inclusive peacekeeping is more likely to be perceived as apolitical, too, and thereby be seen as less imposing on the host state's sovereignty.[71]

In a similar vein, Foradori and Rosa comment that the inclusion of the protection of cultural heritage within their mandate can increase the acceptance of, and support for, peacekeepers. They state that

> [t]hese positive dynamics are in stark contrast to the negative reactions of the local population and rapid disappearance of already tepid support for the international forces in the 2003 Iraq War, after the failure

---

69 Jadranka Petrovic, 'The Cultural Dimension of Peace Operations: Peacekeeping and Cultural Property' in Andrew H Campbell (ed), *Global Leadership Initiatives in Conflict Resolution and Peacebuilding* (IGO Global 2018), 84, 84.
70 Kristel Witkam, 'Cultural Property in Conflict,' *Peace Palace Library Blog*, 4/8/2016 https://www.peacepalacelibrary.nl/2016/08/cultural-property-in-conflict/ accessed 10 November 2019.
71 Jadranka Petrovic, 'The Cultural Dimension of Peace Operations: Peacekeeping and Cultural Property' in Andrew H Campbell (ed), *Global Leadership Initiatives in Conflict Resolution and Peacebuilding* (IGO Global 2018), 84, 88.

to protect cultural property and, in particular, after the looting episode at the Baghdad Museum.[72]

In addition, peacekeepers with a cultural heritage protection mandate can also aid in the stemming of funding created by the looting and selling of artefacts, which finances and fuels conflicts by providing money for armed groups. [73]

The deployment of peacekeeping missions with a cultural heritage protection mandate links to the issue of how cultural heritage is viewed, i.e. as 'belonging' to the local community, from whence the heritage emanates; or as 'belonging' to humankind as whole. In this context, a seminar report of the British Institute of International and Comparative Law comments that 'the cultural property of any people contributes to the cultural heritage of human kind. Thus, loss or damage to such property impoverishes human kind.'[74] Petrovic comments that

> [i]f seen as impartial "protectors" of the "shared" heritage, who by protecting cultural objects concerned (and that way demonstrating cultural awareness, subsuming the significance of such objects to the people of a certain terrain, state, region and humanity), the mission will be perceived in the host state to be less a *xenos*.[75]

This would lead to greater acceptance of the peacekeeping mission locally.

In order to ensure, as far as possible, the success of the cultural heritage element of a peacekeeping mission, the mission should be seen as one aspect of a wider global approach to the protection of cultural heritage. For example, as Foradori and Rosa comment, in order for cultural peacekeeping to have on impact on the looting and smuggling of cultural heritage items, the protection of heritage sites by peacekeepers must be complemented 'with a global policy that addresses the demand side of the destination market, that

---

72 Paolo Foradori and Paolo Rosa, 'Expanding the Peacekeeping Agenda. The Protection of Cultural Heritage in War-Torn Societies' (2017) 29(2) *Global Change, Peace & Security* 145, 154.
73 Ibid., 154.
74 British Institute of International and Comparative Law, *The Protection of Cultural Heritage in Conflict*, Seminar Report (24 April 2013), 3.
75 Jadranka Petrovic, 'The Cultural Dimension of Peace Operations: Peacekeeping and Cultural Property' in Andrew H Campbell (ed), *Global Leadership Initiatives in Conflict Resolution and Peacebuilding* (IGO Global 2018), 84, 88.

is a "market reduction approach" for subduing demand by increasing the risks involved for all parties engaged in illegal trading.'[76]

It is to be noted that the protection of cultural heritage as an aspect of a peacekeeping mission is not an easy task. Cultural heritage sites can have important military and strategic value, leading them to become targets in the first place. As highlighted by Foradori and Rosa, for example, in Iraq and Syria, 'many heritage sites occupy significant locations – on high ground, at important intersections or crossroads, near water – an provide a military strategic advantage that time has not diminished.'[77] Therefore, cultural heritage sites will require 'heavily armed and mandated international forces for their protection.'[78] All mandates which include a cultural heritage protection element must be cognisant of this, and therefore, such peacekeeping missions 'should not at all be conceived and planned as an easy, minor military operation of "light peacekeeping"';[79] rather, it must be recognised that such missions 'will require very robust, properly trained and substantial forces with heavy arms and equipment and capable of performing according to strong rules of engagement spelled out within a solid legal framework.'[80] Indeed, some questions remain unanswered on the issue of the legal framework as it relates to peacekeepers and cultural property. While it is recognised that there is an obligation for peacekeeping forces to respect cultural heritage, it remains uncertain if peacekeepers have an obligation to intervene when other parties to the conflict commit violations. The extent to which peacekeepers can act in defence of cultural heritage must be clearly and unequivocally stated in the peacekeeping mission's mandate.[81]

Foradori and Rosa also point out that interventions by peacekeepers in defence of cultural heritage 'might find it difficult to strike a balance between military necessity and its mandate of cultural protection.'[82] They

---

76 Paolo Foradori and Paolo Rosa, 'Expanding the Peacekeeping Agenda. The Protection of Cultural Heritage in War-Torn Societies' (2017) 29(2) *Global Change, Peace & Security* 145, 160.
77 Ibid., 156.
78 Ibid.
79 Ibid., 157.
80 Ibid.
81 Ibid., 156–157. See also, Jadranka Petrovic, 'The Cultural Dimension of Peace Operations: Peacekeeping and Cultural Property' in Andrew H Campbell (ed), *Global Leadership Initiatives in Conflict Resolution and Peacebuilding* (IGO Global 2018), 84, 84–85, 98; and Roger O'Keefe, 'Protection of Cultural Property under International Law' (2010) 11 *Melbourne Journal of International Law* 1.
82 Paolo Foradori and Paolo Rosa, 'Expanding the Peacekeeping Agenda. The Protection of Cultural Heritage in War-Torn Societies' (2017) 29(2) *Global Change, Peace & Security* 145, 156.

point to the conflicts in Syria and Iraqi, States with significant cultural heritage sites, and state that

> one can easily anticipate scenarios in which cultural heritage protection may be waived on the basis of military necessity or in which cultural protection may contrast or not neatly fit with the military objective of defeating an enemy and securing an area.[83]

While numerous important issues must be taken into consideration in designing a mandate which includes the protection of cultural heritage, it has been suggested that such missions would represent a politically more acceptable form of intervention by the global community and could thus 'gather and sustain international support and mobilization for the mission.'[84] This is because it

> can be presented (and 'marketed') to an internal and/or external audience as an intervention or a very noble, principled, and apolitical goal that unites the international community in contrast to an evil perpetrator who has no justification for committing these destructive deeds. It can also be presented in terms of a just and moral intervention by a global alliance of well-intentioned 'good international citizens' against 'new barbarians' who want to destroy the expressions and symbols of culture and civilization. In short, it is a 'civilization war' against obscurantism and extremism.[85]

However, on the flip side of this argument, support for peacekeeping missions with a cultural heritage protection mandate may wane, depending on the number of casualties suffered by the Mission. If the general public feels that soldiers are dying or being seriously injured as a result of activities to protect cultural heritage, as opposed to human life, its support for such missions could easily and quickly disappear.[86] In this context, it is significant to note that, based on the UN Department of Peacekeeping's data, MINUSMA has suffered significant fatalities, 'which is a considerable reason for concern.'[87]

---

83 Ibid.
84 Ibid, 154.
85 Ibid., 155.
86 Ibid., 157.
87 Jadranka Petrovic, 'The Cultural Dimension of Peace Operations: Peacekeeping and Cultural Property' in Andrew H Campbell (ed), *Global Leadership Initiatives in Conflict Resolution and Peacebuilding* (IGO Global 2018), 84, 98. As of September 2019, there

Another concern which has been raised in the context of cultural peacekeeping initiatives is the difficulty in managing the different sets of expertise required for a successful mission, including archaeologists, historians, and anthropologists, given that 'cooperation can be particularly challenging between diverse working communities with very different educational backgrounds, mindsets, training, sensibilities, work habits, and customs.'[88]

The most significant risk involved in deploying a peacekeeping mission with a cultural heritage protection mandate has, however, been identified as creating a 'clash of civilizations' between the international community in the guise of the peacekeepers and an armed group, such as ISIS. If the peacekeepers are not well trained in the culture of the State in which they intervene and do not pay due respect to its heritage, they can be portrayed as neo-colonisers or invaders, thus escalating the conflict, especially if the peacekeepers are from Western States.[89] Such situations could be manipulated to the advantage of Islamic fundamentalist groups and feed into their narrative of Western colonialism. Thus, peacekeeping missions with a cultural heritage protection mandate 'must be very carefully handled to avoid letting the adversary manipulate it to its own advantage.'[90]

In sum, peacekeeping missions with a cultural heritage protection mandate can, potentially, have numerous positive outcomes which can not only help to implement the legal framework on the protection of cultural property, but also help the implementation of the broader peacekeeping mandate. However, cultural peacekeeping is a multidimensional and multilayered operation, and thus

> should not be mistaken for nor presented to the public as a minor, light, and inexpensive intervention, be it in economic terms or in terms of possible human loss. Quite the opposite, it is an extremely complex and politically sensitive military exercise that needs careful planning and adequate capabilities,

and its mismanagement could 'severely backfire.'[91]

---

were 204 fatalities from among MINUSMA, https://peacekeeping.un.org/en/mission/minusma accessed 10 November 2019.
88 Paolo Foradori and Paolo Rosa, 'Expanding the peacekeeping agenda. The protection of cultural heritage in war-torn societies' (2017) 29(2) *Global Change, Peace & Security* 145, 157.
89 Ibid., 158.
90 Ibid., 159.
91 Ibid.

UNESCO initiatives

UNESCO fully supports the integration of a cultural heritage protection mandate into peacekeeping activities, and at its General Conference in 2015, it passed a resolution, proposed by Italy, to establish the 'Blue Helmets for Culture.'[92] This resolution supports the Director General's efforts aimed at embedding the protection of cultural heritage and cultural diversity in humanitarian action, global security strategies, and peacebuilding processes. It also incorporates a six-year strategy, the Strategy for the Reinforcement of UNESCO's Action for the Protection of Culture and the Promotion of Cultural Pluralism in the Event of Armed Conflict, which is aimed at protecting cultural and promoting cultural diversity in the context of armed conflict.[93] This strategy, according to Jakubowski,

> has two objectives: to strengthen UNESCO Member States' ability to prevent, mitigate, and recover the loss of cultural heritage and diversity as a result of armed conflict; and to incorporate the protection of culture into humanitarian actions, security strategies, and peace-building processes.[94]

It builds on work done by MINUSMA, and is based on two main pillars, i.e. the creation of an expert task force in the area of cultural heritage, which can be rapidly mobilised and cooperate with UNESCO to effectively implement the relevant international legal framework for the protection of cultural heritage during and after armed conflict; and the incorporation of cultural elements in peacekeeping mandates for forces deployed in locations where cultural heritage is at risk. At the adoption of the Strategy, the General Conference of UNESCO requested the elaboration, in coordination with Member States and relevant actors, of an Action Plan to further refine and implement the Strategy. In addition, mechanisms for the rapid response and mobilisation of national experts were to be defined and practical ways for the implementation of such mechanisms were to be explored. Work is continuing on implementing this Strategy and on creating a compressive and multifaceted response to the destruction of cultural heritage

---

92 UNESCO Resolution 38 C/48 (2015). See https://www.theheritagealliance.org.uk/update/unesco-agrees-to-blue-helmets-of-culture/ accessed 10 November 2019.
93 The text of the Strategy is available at: https://en.unesco.org/system/files/235186e1.pdfaccessed 10 November 2019.
94 Andrzej Jakubowski, 'Resolution 2347: Mainstreaming the Protection of Cultural Heritage at the Global Level' (2018) 48 *Questions of International Law* 21, 32.

during armed conflict, including the training of peacekeepers in the field of cultural heritage.[95]

This initiative has been supported by an agreement signed by UNESCO and the Italian government in 2016 for the establishment of an Italian Task Force, which is based on the Italian Carabinieri Command for the Protection of Cultural Heritage. UNESCO has urged other States to follow the lead of Italy in this regard, with former Director General Bokova stating that 'this Task Force, and the agreement signed in Rome with the Italian Government, will become a model for other countries.'[96] A welcome advance has been the recent establishment of a Cultural Property Protection Unit within the British Armed Forces[97] and a Cultural Heritage Task Force within the US Armed Forces.[98]

---

95 Paragraph 35 of the Strategy states: 'Cooperation with the military will be further developed, including with United Nations peacekeeping forces, to enhance knowledge and understanding of international humanitarian law related to the protection of cultural heritage during conflict. UNESCO will build on the positive experience of the implementation of United Nations Security Council Resolution 2100 (2013) that established the United Nations Multidimensional Integrated Stabilization Mission in Mali (MINUSMA) and requested it to ensure the safeguarding of cultural heritage sites in collaboration with UNESCO. In particular, the integration of a module on the protection of cultural heritage and diversity within the standard training of peace-keeping forces will be proposed. Ultimately, it is hoped that increased awareness of the military on international humanitarian cultural heritage law will lead to the operationalization of protected cultural areas in zones of conflict; that is significant cultural heritage sites, which are clearly identified and protected from the conflict based on a mutual agreement between military forces operating in the given area.' See Paolo Foradori and Paolo Rosa, 'Expanding the Peacekeeping Agenda. The Protection of Cultural Heritage in War-Torn Societies' (2017) 29(2) *Global Change, Peace & Security* 145, 153.
96 UNESCO, 'UNESCO Director-General: "Protecting Culture is a Moral Responsibility and a Security Issue"' (16 February 2016) http://www.unesco.org/new/en/media-services/single-view/news/unesco_director_general_protecting_culture_is_a_moral_resp/ accessed 10 November 2019. See also, UNESCO, 'Italy Creates a UNESCO Emergency Task Force for Culture' (16 February 2016) http://whc.unesco.org/en/news/1436/ accessed 10 November 2019.
97 '"Monuments Men": New Army Unit to Protect Ancient Treasures,' *Forces Network* (31 January 2019), https://www.forces.net/news/military-wants-reservists-indiana-jones-fl air-new-unit accessed 10 November 2019. See NATO, 'The Protection of Cultural Property in the Event of Armed Conflict: Unnecessary Distraction or Mission Relevant Priority?' (NATO OPEN Publications 2018).
98 'US Army Creates Cultural Heritage Task Force,' *Artforum* (22 October 2019) https://www.artforum.com/news/us-army-creates-cultural-heritage-task-force-81101 accessed 10 November 2019.

Peacebuilding and sustainable development

Within the context of the securitisation of cultural heritage, significant emphasis has been placed on the role which cultural heritage can play in peacebuilding and in the creation of post-conflict sustainable development. Foradori and Rosa highlight that as hostilities draw to a close, cultural peacekeeping can 'help to ensure quicker recovery and stabilization by promoting societal and economic regeneration for a long-lasting peace.'[99] This, to an extent, is also linked with the deployment of cultural peacekeeping missions, and, indeed, the responsibility to rebuild aspects of the R2P doctrine.

Bokova clearly linked the securitisation of cultural heritage with peacebuilding, stating that '[t]he conclusion is clear: culture is at the front line of modern conflict. This requires us to rethink the importance of culture in peacebuilding.'[100] With regard to the situation in Iraq, Bokova further emphasised the importance of cultural heritage for a peaceful future, stating that cultural heritage is 'a key to resilience for building a better future.'[101] This link between the protection of cultural property and peacebuilding has also been highlighted in a report by the British Institute of International and Comparative Law, which states that '[a]s cultural property reflects the life, history and identity of the community, its preservation helps to rebuild a broken community, re-establish its identity, and link its past with its present and future.'[102] In a similar vein, former UN Secretary General Ban Ki-moon stated that the protection of cultural heritage has become a 'political and security imperative' which should translate into a 'central component of peacebuilding and conflict resolution efforts and humanitarian and development policies.'[103]

Once a conflict is over, on a purely practical level, the survival of cultural heritage can help to contribute to a return to economic security and

---

99 Paolo Foradori and Paolo Rosa, 'Expanding the Peacekeeping Agenda. The Protection of Cultural Heritage in War-Torn Societies' (2017) 29(2) *Global Change, Peace & Security* 145, 154.
100 Irina Bokova, 'Culture on the Front Line of New Wars' (2015) XXII(1) *Brown Journal of World Affairs* 289, 289–290.
101 UNESCO, 'The Director-General of UNESCO Irina Bokova calls on Iraqis to Stand United and Protect their Cultural Heritage' http://en.unesco.org/news/director-general-unesco-irina-bokova-calls-iraqis-stand-united-around-their-cultural-heritage accessed 10 November 2019.
102 British Institute of International and Comparative Law, *The Protection of Cultural Heritage in Conflict*, Seminar Report (24 April 2013), 3.
103 Statement by UN secretary-general Ban Ki-moon, in UNESCO, 'Background note to the International Conference "Heritage and Cultural Diversity at Risk in Iraq and Syria" – The Protection of Heritage and Cultural Diversity: A Humanitarian and Security Imperative in the Conflicts of the 21st Century,' UNESCO Headquarters, Paris (3 December 2014), 5.

post-conflict income generation from tourism.[104] In addition, in post-conflict societies, cultural heritage can become a unifying symbol for communities and can support them 'to break the cycle of violence and heal the scars of war.'[105] Therefore, the importance of its protection during armed conflict is heightened. UNESCO has stated that

> the destruction of cultural heritage weakens a community's capacity for resilience and recovery and makes post-conflict reconciliation much more difficult. Conversely, the rehabilitation of cultural heritage, in the post-conflict stage, may play a decisive role in rebuilding the fabric of societies and in creating the foundations for long-lasting peace and security.[106]

The importance of cultural heritage to the essence of societal identity means that its survival throughout a conflict can help to support the survival of the societal group post-conflict. Thus, cultural heritage has been recognised by the UN General Assembly as one of the over-arching principles of sustainable development in its '2030 Agenda for Sustainable Development,'[107] adopted in 2015.

Conclusion

There may be some resistance to the broadening of the scope of the concept of a threat to peace and security to include destruction of cultural heritage.[108] The move to include threats to health, such as the Ebola crisis in

---

104 Paolo Foradori and Paolo Rosa, 'Expanding the Peacekeeping Agenda. The Protection of Cultural Heritage in War-Torn Societies' (2017) 29(2) *Global Change, Peace & Security* 145, 154.
105 UNESCO, Report of the International Conference 'Heritage and Cultural Diversity at Risk in Iraq and Syria' (2014), 24, http://www.unesco.org/culture/pdf/iraq-syria/IraqSyriaReport-en.pdf accessed 10 November 2019.
106 Ibid.
107 'Transforming Our World: The 2030 Agenda for Sustainable Development' UNGA Res 70/1 (21 October 2015) UN Doc A/RES/70/1.
108 In relation to the question of what constitutes a threat to international peace and security, see Hikaru Yamashita, 'Reading "Threats to International Peace and Security," 1946–2005' (2007) 18(3) *Diplomacy & Statecraft* 551; Oli Brown and Robert McLeman, 'A Recurring Anarchy? The Emergence of Climate Change as a Threat to International Peace and Security' (2009) 9(3) *Conflict, Security & Development* 289; and Ian Hurd, 'The Selectively Expansive UN Security Council: Domestic Threats to Peace and Security' (2012) 106 *Proceedings of the Annual Meeting (American Society of International Law)* 35.

2014,[109] encountered some criticism.[110] However, the UN Security Council has clearly endorsed a security paradigm within which the protection of cultural heritage is viewed. In addition to the various Security Council resolutions underlining this approach, discussed here, the General Assembly has also linked the destruction of cultural heritage with peace and security. In 2015, for example, the Assembly stated that the 'destruction of cultural heritage, which is representative of the diversity of human culture, erases the collective memories of a nation, destabilizes communities and threatens their cultural identity,' and emphasised the importance of 'cultural diversity and pluralism as well as freedom of religion and belief for achieving peace, stability, reconciliation and social cohesion.'[111]

The trend towards securitisation has been embraced not only by the UN, but also by other organisations and in academia. UNESCO, as highlighted above, has clearly supported the securitisation move through its adoption of a Strategy for the Reinforcement of UNESCO's Action for the Protection of Culture and the Promotion of Cultural Pluralism in the Event of Armed Conflict, which is aimed at protecting culture and promoting cultural diversity in the context of armed conflict.[112] Foradori and Rosa thus comment that the 'endorsement of the securitization of cultural heritage destruction by the United Nations ... has appealed to the international community of states to activate exceptional measures to address the threat.'[113] The peace and security framework has allowed for a variety of approaches to the protection of cultural property to be intertwined in a global strategy and has provided the UN and other organisations, such as UNESCO, with additional tools to address cultural heritage destruction. While the destruction of cultural heritage continues to be an issue in some places around the world, the security paradigm highlights its importance to the global community and enhances opportunities for its protection.

---

109 UN SC Resolution 2177 (18 September 2014).
110 Charlotte Steinorth, 'The Security Council's Response to the Ebola Crisis: A Step Forward or Backwards in the Realization of the Right to Health?,' *EJIL: Talk!* (2 March 2017) https://www.ejiltalk.org/the-security-councils-response-to-the-ebola-crisis-a-step-forward-or-backwards-in-the-realization-of-the-right-to-health/ accessed 10 November 2019; Gary Wilson, 'Collective Security, "Threats to the Peace," and the Ebola Outbreak' (2015) 6(1) *Journal of Philosophy of International Law* 1; and Alison Agnew, 'A Combative Disease: The Ebola Epidemic in International Law' (2016) 39(1) *Boston College International and Comparative Law Review* 97.
111 UNGA Res 69/281 (28 May 2015).
112 The text of the Strategy is available at https://en.unesco.org/system/files/235186e1.pdf accessed 10 November 2019.
113 Paolo Foradori and Paolo Rosa, 'Expanding the peacekeeping agenda. The protection of cultural heritage in war-torn societies' (2017) 29(2) *Global Change, Peace and Security* 145, 152.

Conclusion

Cultural heritage has been the victim of numerous devastating attacks during recent armed conflicts in the Middle East and North Africa. While this is not a new occurrence, as history abounds with various examples of destruction of cultural heritage during war, these attacks were hallmarked with a frequency and severity never previously witnessed. Museums were destroyed, mausoleums razed, and monuments demolished across the region, as fundamentalist Islamic groups viewed cultural heritage sites and artefacts as legitimate targets, representing a history and identity to be destroyed.

This destruction of cultural heritage was perpetrated in spite of the extant legal framework seeking to protect heritage during armed conflict, which, as this book has shown, is contained in a variety of legal instruments. The recent unrelenting and repeated destruction of cultural heritage in places such as Iraq, Syria, and Mali has illustrated the weakness of the framework. The ferocity of the destruction and the significant losses incurred in recent attacks focused the world's attention on the issue, and engendered discussions on how better to tackle the problem of destruction of cultural heritage during armed conflict. This book has sought to, first, identify the extant legal framework which seeks to protect cultural heritage during armed conflict and analyse its development over time; and second, to investigate other paradigms which may provide additional protection for cultural heritage under attack.

Chapter 1 provided an analysis of the development of the legal framework on the protection of cultural heritage during armed conflict, starting with a discussion of how the destruction of cultural heritage was viewed in ancient civilisations, as well as by the early writers on public international law, such as Grotius and de Vattel. The chapter then identified how the international legal framework first approached the issue of the protection of cultural heritage in 19th-century instruments such as the Lieber Code 1883 and the Hague Regulations 1899. This early legal framework sought to protect cultural sites, such as museums, during armed conflict by prohibiting attacks on them as a result of their status as civilian objects,

88 Conclusion

which should be distinguished from military objectives under the fundamental international humanitarian law principle of distinction.[1] Thus, the prohibition of attacks on museums was often included in provisions which also prohibited attacks on other civilian objects and places, such as hospitals and educational institutions.[2] This approach, described by Frulli as the 'civilian use'[3] paradigm to the protection of cultural heritage, continued into the 20th century with the Hague Conventions of 1907, for example.[4] However, with the development of an international human rights discourse after World War II, and notably the adoption of the Universal Declaration of Human Rights (UDHR) in 1948, heritage issues began to be viewed as part of the cultural rights paradigm, and cultural artefacts and sites were recognised as being worthy of protection, not merely because of their status as civilian objects, but also because of their inherent value to communities and humanity at large. Thus, attacks on cultural heritage during armed conflict were prohibited based on what Frulli called a 'culture-value' rationale.[5] This paradigm is reflected in the 1954 Hague Convention and its protocols.[6] The United Nations Educational, Scientific and Cultural Organization (UNESCO)

---

1 International Committee of the Red Cross Customary IHL Rule 7 states: 'The parties to the conflict must at all times distinguish between civilian objects and military objectives. Attacks may only be directed against military objectives. Attacks must not be directed against civilian objects.' Jean-Marie Henckaerts and Louise Doswald-Beck (eds), *Customary Humanitarian Law. Volume I: Rules* (ICRC/Cambridge University Pres 2005). See Customary IHL Database https://www.icrc.org/en/war-and-law/treaties-customary-law/customary-law accessed 10 November 2019.

2 See, for example, Article 34 Instructions for the Government of Armies of the United States in the Field. Prepared by Francis Lieber, promulgated as General Orders No. 100 by President Lincoln, 24 April 1863; and Articles 27, Convention II with Respect to the Laws and Customs of War on Land and its annex: Regulations concerning the Laws and Customs of War on Land, 1899. Annex to the Convention; Regulations respecting the Laws and Customs of War on Land.

3 See Michaela Frulli, 'The Criminalization of Offences against Cultural Heritage in Times of Armed Conflict: The Quest for Consistency' (2011) 22(1) *European Journal of International Law* (2011) 203.

4 See Article 27 of the Regulations annexed to Hague Convention IV with Respect to the Laws and Customs of War on Land, 1907; and Article 5 of Hague Convention IX concerning Bombardment by Naval Forces in Time of War, 1907.

5 Michaela Frulli, 'The Criminalization of Offences against Cultural Heritage in Times of Armed Conflict: The Quest for Consistency' (2011) 22(1) *European Journal of International Law* (2011) 203.

6 Convention for the Protection of Cultural Property in the Event of Armed Conflict, adopted at The Hague, 1954, 249 UNTS 240. First Protocol to the Convention for the Protection of Cultural Property in the Event of Armed Conflict 1954, adopted at The Hague, 14 May 1954, 249 UNTS 358. Second Protocol to the Convention for the Protection of Cultural Property in the Event of Armed Conflict 1954, adopted at The Hague, 26 March 1999, 2252 UNTS 172.

Conclusion 89

further developed the 'culture-value' paradigm on the protection of cultural heritage with the adoption of a number of instruments highlighting the importance of culture to humanity as a whole, including instruments which apply in times of peace as well as war, such as the World Heritage Convention 1972.[7] This chapter also discussed how the international legal framework has included provisions on individual criminal responsibility for attacks on cultural heritage, with such attacks being categorised as war crimes in the statutes of international criminal tribunals, including the International Criminal Tribunal for the Former Yugoslavia (ICTY)[8] and the International Criminal Court (ICC).[9] This discussion illustrated how, although the international criminal tribunal statutes form part of the 'civilian use' paradigm on the protection of cultural heritage, international jurisprudence has taken a much more expansive view of the importance and value of cultural heritage to local communities and to the global community.[10] Ultimately, the chapter concluded that despite the multifarious legal instruments which seek to protect cultural heritage during armed conflict, whether based on the 'civilian use' or 'culture-value' paradigm, a different paradigm is required in the face of the recent attacks on heritage in the Middle East and North Africa.

Chapter 2 provided an analysis of proposals for other paradigms which could be utilised for the protection of cultural heritage during armed conflict recently offered in academia and by international bodies: cultural cleansing, the Responsibility to Protect (R2P) doctrine, and cultural genocide. It assessed the potential of each of these paradigms to provide additional protection to cultural heritage. The label 'cultural cleansing', as noted in this chapter, was frequently used to describe the recent attacks on cultural heritage by the Islamic State of Iraq and Syria (ISIS) and other fundamentalist groups by the then Director General of UNESCO, Irina Bokova. The label illustrated that attacks on cultural heritage were not mere attacks on civilian objects, but were also attacks on the history, memory, and identity of communities, which would impact future generations. While the label is emotive and was successful in focusing global attention on the destruction of cultural sites and artefacts in the Middle East and North Africa, it lacks a solid legal basis, and thus would not be a very effective paradigm

7 World Heritage Convention Concerning the Protection of the World Cultural and Natural Heritage, adopted at Paris, 16 November 1972.
8 Article 3(d) Statute of the International Criminal Tribunal of the Former Yugoslavia as established by Security Council Resolution 827 (1993).
9 Article 8(2)(b)(ix) and Article 8(2)(e)(iv) Statute of the International Criminal Court (1998), 2187 UNTS 90.
10 For example, see *Prosecutor v Kordić and Čerzek,* IT-95-14/2-A, *Prosecutor v Kristić* IT-98-33-T, and *Prosecutor v Al Mahdi,* ICC-01/12-01/15.

Conclusion

through which to view the protection of cultural heritage during armed conflict. Cultural cleansing does, however, echo the concept of ethnic cleansing, which falls within the R2P doctrine, and indeed, the R2P doctrine has been identified as a potentially important paradigm for the protection of cultural heritage within academia.[11] The chapter thus next assessed if the R2P doctrine could apply to situations of cultural heritage destruction. While, in theory, this is possible – both during armed conflict and, indeed, in times of peace – and the idea that the international community should have an obligation to intervene to protect cultural property when States are unwilling or unable to do so is an attractive one, given the lack of enthusiasm for the R2P doctrine and the vagueness which still exists with regard to its contours, and, indeed, legal status, it is doubtful if the doctrine would be an effective paradigm for the protection of cultural heritage. The final potential paradigm for the protection of cultural heritage during armed conflict assessed in this chapter is that of cultural genocide. This is linked with the previous paradigm, as the R2P doctrine is triggered by acts of war crimes, crimes against humanity, ethnic cleansing, and genocide.[12] The chapter discussed the Genocide Convention of 1948,[13] and how the definition of the crime of genocide which was included in this instrument, and subsequently replicated in numerous other legal instruments, excluded the concept of cultural genocide from its scope.[14] It illustrated how this departs from Lemkin's original understanding of the crime,[15] and discussed how some attempts have been made over the years since the adoption of the Genocide Convention to revive the concept of cultural genocide, including in respect of the destruction of cultural heritage.[16] It was concluded, however, that,

---

11 See Federico Lenzerini, 'Terrorism, Conflicts and the Responsibility to Protect Cultural Heritage' (2016) 51(2) *The International Spectator* 70; and Thomas G Weiss and Nina Connelly, 'Cultural Cleansing and Mass Atrocities', J Paul Getty Trust Occasional Papers, No. 1 (2017), 6. See also Edward C Luck, 'Cultural Genocide and the Protection of Cultural Heritage', J Paul Getty Trust Occasional Papers in Cultural Heritage Policy, Number 2 (2018), 15.
12 Report of the International Commission on Intervention and State Sovereignty (2001) http://responsibilitytoprotect.org/ICISS%20Report.pdf accessed 10 November 2019.
13 Convention on the Prevention and Punishment of the Crime of Genocide, opened for signature 9 December 1948, 78 UNTS 277.
14 See Elise Novic, *The Concept of Cultural Genocide* (Oxford University Press 2016).
15 Raphael Lemkin, *Axis Rule in Occupied Europe: Laws of Occupation, Analysis of Government, and Proposals for Redress* (Carnegie Endowment for International Peace 1944).
16 See, for example, Edward C Luck, 'Cultural Genocide and the Protection of Cultural Heritage', J Paul Getty Trust Occasional Papers in Cultural Heritage Policy, Number 2 (2018)

Conclusion 91

given the determinations on this topic by the ICTY[17] and the International Law Commission,[18] it is improbable that the concept of cultural genocide would be an effective paradigm to further the protection of cultural heritage.

Finally, Chapter 3 focused on recent developments in the United Nations (UN) and other international bodies which have advanced the discourse and practice on the protection of cultural heritage during armed conflict within a security paradigm. The UN, via Resolutions, has linked attacks on cultural heritage with the financing of terrorism, the fuelling of conflict, and destruction of community identity and the disruption of society, and thus has identified it as a threat to international peace and security. The chapter analysed UN Security Council Resolutions which focused on attacks on cultural heritage and discussed UN and UNESCO initiatives in the field of cultural heritage, particularly the development of cultural peacekeeping, which firmly places the protection of cultural heritage within a security paradigm. It is concluded that this paradigm has the potential to support the extant legal framework and to offer additional protection for cultural property during armed conflict.

While the current legal framework is not without its problems, it is still important that States which have not yet ratified the core international instruments dealing with heritage, including the 1954 Convention and its Protocols as well as the 1972 World Heritage Convention and the 1995 UNIDROIT Convention, do so. In addition, they should also ratify the Rome Statute and adopt domestic legislation to facilitate the prosecution of crimes against cultural heritage. A number of domestic legal systems do allow for the prosecution of crimes against cultural heritage. In Syria, for example, the Syrian Antiquities Law of 26 October 1963, passed under Decree Law No 222 (Syrian Antiquities Law), allows for individual criminal responsibility in respect of such crimes.[19] The strengthening of the reach and implementation of the legal framework will hopefully result in an increase in protection of cultural heritage worldwide and a decrease in impunity for crimes against culture.

As stated, recent conflicts have witnessed significant damage to cultural sites and artefacts. However, some successes in the protection of cultural heritage are to be noted. In Egypt in 2011, for example, cultural sites and artefacts were essentially spared from damage as the local community created

---

17 See *Prosecutor v Kristić (Judgment)*, IT-98-33-T, 2 August 2001, para. 580.
18 See Report of the International Law Commission on the Work of its Forty-Eighth Session, UN Doc A/51/10, 90–91.
19 Institute for National Security and Counterterrorism, Syracuse University, "'Chautauqua Blueprint' to Prosecute Syrian War Crimes Unveiled", 3 October 2013 http://insct.syr.edu /chautauqua-blueprint-prosecute-syrian-war-crimes-unveiled/ accessed 10 November 2019.

human chains around the museums in Cairo.[20] Also, in the aftermath of the conflict in Libya, 'careful curatorial storage of the Tripoli museum and some restraint on the part of the coalition forces facilitated by information networks prevented the destruction and looting that might have otherwise occurred.'[21] In addition, despite the significant loss of life in the Afghanistan conflict, the artefacts housed in the Kabul Museum were protected.[22]

In order to build on these small successes, it is necessary that a multi-dimensional and multilayered approach to the protection of cultural heritage be adopted. The refocusing of global attention on cultural heritage as a result of recent attacks in the Middle East and North Africa has triggered a new discourse and suggestions as to how best heritage can be protected. As Cuno comments,

> [a]ny international response must include these three tactics: intervening in conflict zones before damage and destruction have taken place; engaging and supporting local authorities in the protection of sites and heritage; and avoiding symbolic gestures in favour of real, concrete measures. But for this strategy to succeed, it must include something more: a broad legal and diplomatic framework that draws upon precedents to which the international community is committed.[23]

However, international responses are urgently needed. The protection of cultural heritage must be recognised as a priority by the international community; in sum, 'we need to defend culture – a source of resilience and resistance, of belonging and identity – as a wellspring to rebuild and restore normality in societies in crisis.'[24] Reflecting this idea, an inscription outside the National Museum of Afghanistan states that 'a nation stays alive when its culture stays alive.'[25] It is therefore incumbent on the international community to continue to further develop effective paradigms to protect cultural heritage for the good of society and future generations.

---

20 See British Institute of International and Comparative Law, 'The Protection of Cultural Heritage in Conflict', Seminar Report, 24 April 2013, 4.
21 Ibid.
22 Ibid.
23 James Cuno, 'The Responsibility to Protect the World's Cultural Heritage', 23 *Brown J World Affairs* (2016) 97, 10.
24 Irina Bokova, 'Culture on the Front Line of New Wars', 22(1) *Brown Journal of World Affairs* (2015) 289, 294.
25 British Council, 'A Nation Stays Alive when its Culture Stays Alive', https://www.britishcouncil.org/research-policy-insight/insight-articles/a-nation-stays-alive accessed 10 November 2019.

Bibliography

Hirad Abtathi, 'The Protection of Cultural Property in Times of Armed Conflict: The Practice of the International Criminal Tribunal for the Former Yugoslavia' (2001) 14 *Harvard Human Rights Journal* 1.

African Commission on Human and Peoples' Rights, 'Press Release on the Destruction of Cultural and Ancient Monuments in the Malian City of Timbuktu' (10 July 2012) http://www.achpr.org/press/2012/07/d115/ accessed 10 November 2019.

African Union, 'Solemn Declaration on Situation in Mali' (19 July 2012) http://www.wacsi.org/en/site/newsroom/1410/AU-COLEMN-DECLARATION-ON-THE-SITUATION-IN-MALI-African-Union accessed 10 November 2019.

Alison Agnew, 'A Combative Disease: The Ebola Epidemic in International Law' (2016) 39(1) *Boston College International and Comparative Law Review* 97.

Kofi A Annan, 'We the Peoples. The Role of the United Nations in the 21st Century' (2000) 48 https://www.un.org/en/events/pastevents/pdfs/We_The_Peoples.pdf.

A Azoulay, 'Historic Milestone for the Protection of Cultural Heritage' (24 March 2017) https://onu.delegfrance.org/Historic-milestone-for-the-protection-of-cultural-heritage.

Francesco Badarin, 'Editorial' (2001) May–June *The World Heritage Newsletter* 1.

Raymond Baker, Shereen Ismael and Tareq Ismael, *Cultural Cleansing in Iraq. Why Museums Were Looted, Libraries Burned and Academics Murdered* (Pluto Press, 2009).

Marc Balcells, 'Left Behind? Cultural Destruction, the Role of the International Criminal Tribunal for the Former Yugoslavia in Deterring it and Cultural Heritage Prevention Policies in the Aftermath of the Balkan Wars' (2015) 21(1) *European Journal on Criminal Policy and Research* 1.

Alina Balta and Nadia Banteka, 'The Al-Mahdi Reparations Order at the ICC: A Step towards Justice for Victims of Crimes against Cultural Heritage' *Opinio Juris*, 6 September 2017.

Irina Bokova, 'Culture on the Front Line of New Wars' (2015) 22 *Brown Journal of World Affairs* 289.

Irina Bokova, 'United Nations Security Council Resolution 2347' (24 March 2017) UNESCO Doc. CL/4210.

Bibliography

Whitney Bren, 'Terrorists and Antiquities: Lessons from the Destruction of the Bamiyan Buddhas, Current ISIS Aggression, and a Proposed Framework for Cultural Property Crimes' (2016) 34(1) *Cardozo Arts & Entertainment Law Journal* 215.

Bureau of Educational and Cultural Affairs, 'Secretary of State Kerry and Director General Bokova Call for End to Cultural Destruction in Iraq and Syria' (nd) http://www.unesco.org/new/en/member-states/single-view/news/state_secretary_kerry_and_director_general_bokova_call_for_e/ accessed 10 November 2019.

British Council, 'A Nation Stays Alive when its Culture Stays Alive' (2017) https://www.britishcouncil.org/research-policy-insight/insight-articles/a-nation-stays-alive accessed 10 November 2019.

British Institute of International and Comparative Law, 'The Protection of Cultural Heritage in Conflict', Seminar Report, (24 April 2013).

Sarah Brockmeier, Oliver Stuenkel and Marcos Tourino, 'The Impact of the Libya Intervention Debates on Norms of Protection' (2016) 30(1) *Global Society* 134.

Oli Brown and Robert McLeman, 'A Recurring Anarchy? The Emergence of Climate Change as a Threat to International Peace and Security' (2009) 9(3) *Conflict, Security & Development* 289.

Jason Burke, 'ICC Ruling for Timbuktu Destruction 'Should be Deterrent to Others'' *The Guardian*, 27 September 2016.

Barry Buzan, Ole Waever and Japp de Wilde, *Security: A New Framework for Analysis* (Lynne Rienner 1998).

Commission on the Responsibility of the Authors of the War and on Enforcement of Penalties, 'Report Presented to the Preliminary Peace Conference' (1920) 14 *American Journal of International Law* 95, 115.

James Cuno, 'The Responsibility to Protect the World's Cultural Heritage' (2016) 23 *Brown Journal of World Affairs* 97.

Hugh Eakin, 'Use Force to Stop ISIS' Destruction of Art and History', *New York Times*, 3 April 2015.

Mohamed Elewa Badar and Noelle Higgins, 'Discussion Interrupted: The Destruction and Protection of Cultural Property under International Law and Islamic Law - the Case of *Prosecutor v. Al Mahdi*' (2017) 17(3) *International Criminal Law Review* 486.

Mohamed Elewa Badar and Noelle Higgins, 'The Destruction of Cultural Property in Timbuktu: Challenging the ICC War Crime Paradigm' (2017) 74(3/4) *Europa Ethnica* 99.

European Parliament, 'Resolution on Syria of 19 June 2015 and Resolution on the Destruction of Cultural Sites Perpetrated by ISIS/Da'esh' (30 April 2015).

Foreign and Commonwealth Office and Peter Wilson CMG, 'UK Mission to the United Nations, New York, Statement by Ambassador Peter Wilson, UK Deputy Permanent Representative to the United Nations, at the Security Council briefing on Protecting Cultural Heritage' (24 March 2017).

Paolo Foradori and Paolo Rosa, 'Expanding the Peacekeeping Agenda: The Protection of Cultural Heritage in War-Torn Societies' (2017) 29(2) *Global Change, Peace and Security* 145.

Bibliography 95

Francesco Francioni and Federico Lenzerini, 'The Destruction of the Buddhas of Bamiyan and International Law' (2003) 14(4) *European Journal of International Law* 619.

Francesco Francioni and Federico Lenzerini, 'The Obligation to Prevent and Avoid Destruction of Cultural Heritage: From Bamiyan to Iraq', in Barbara T. Hoffman (ed), *Art and Cultural Heritage* (Cambridge University Press 2006), 28.

Francesco Francioni and Christine Bakker, 'Responsibility to Protect, Humanitarian Intervention and Human Rights: Lessons from Libya to Mali', Transworld Working Paper Number 15, (2013) http://www.transworld-fp7.eu/?p=1138 accessed 10 November 2019.

Donna-Lee Frieze (ed), *Totally Unofficial: The Autobiography of Raphael Lemkin* (Yale University Press 2013).

Manlio Frigo, 'Cultural Property v. Cultural Heritage: A "Battle of Concepts" in International Law?' (2004) 86(854) *International Review of the Red Cross* 367.

Michaela Frulli, 'The Criminalization of Offences against Cultural Heritage in Times of Armed Conflict: The Quest for Consistency' (2011) 22(1) *European Journal of International Law* 203.

Hugo Grotius, trans by AC Campbell, *The Rights of War and Peace, Including the Law of Nature and of Nations* (M Walter Dunne 1901), Book III, Chapter XII.

Kristin Hausler, 'Cultural Heritage and the Security Council: Why Resolution 2347 Matters' (2018) 48 *Question of International Law* 5.

Jean-Marie Henckaerts and Louise Doswald-Beck (eds), *Customary Humanitarian Law. Volume I: Rules* (ICRC/Cambridge University Press 2005). See Customary IHL Database https://www.icrc.org/en/war-and-law/treaties-customary-law/customary-law accessed 10 November 2019.

Human Rights and Equal Opportunity Commission, *Report of the National Inquiry into the Separation of Aboriginal and Torres Strait Islander Children from their Families*. Human Rights and Equal Opportunity Commission, (1997).

Ian Hurd, 'The Selectively Expansive UN Security Council: Domestic Threats to Peace and Security' (2012) 106 *Proceedings of the Annual Meeting* (American Society of International Law) 35.

ICC Office of the Prosecutor, *Strategic Plan 2019–2021* (17 July 2019) available at during the Strategic Plan 2019–2021 https://www.icc-cpi.int/itemsDocuments/20190726-strategic-plan-eng.pdf accessed 10 November 2019.

ICISS, 'Report of the International Commission on Intervention and State Sovereignty' (2001) http://responsibilitytoprotect.org/ICISS%20Report.pdf.

Andrzej Jakubowski, 'Resolution 2347: Mainstreaming the Protection of Cultural Heritage at the Global Level' (2018) 48 *Questions of International Law* 21.

Joint Declaration of the Ministers of Culture of G& on the Occasion of the Meeting, 'Culture as an Instrument for Dialogue among Peoples' (30–31 March 2017).

J Karlsrud, 'The UN at War: Examining the Consequences of Peace-Enforcement Mandates for the UN Peacekeeping Operations in the CAR, the DRC and Mali' (2015) 36(1) *Third World Quarterly* 40.

John Kerry, *Remarks at Threats to Cultural Heritage in Iraq and Syria* (22 September 2014) http://www.state.gov/secretary/remarks/2014/09/231992htm accessed 10 November 2019.

Bibliography

Benjamin Lambert, *NATO's Air War for Kosovo: A Strategic and Operational Assessment* (Rand 2001).

Raphael Lemkin, *Axis Rule in Occupied Europe: Laws of Occupation, Analysis of Government, and Proposals for Redress* (Carnegie Endowment for International Peace 1944).

Federico Lenzerini, 'Terrorism, Conflicts and the Responsibility to Protect Cultural Heritage' (2016) 51(2) *The International Spectator* 70.

Marina Lostal, 'Syria's World Cultural Heritage and Individual Criminal Responsibility' (2015) 3 *International Review of Law* http://dx.doi.org/10.5339/irl.2015.3 accessed 1 November 2019.

Marina Lostal, *International Cultural Heritage Law in Armed Conflict* (Cambridge University Press 2017), 3.

Edward C Luck, 'Cultural Genocide and the Protection of Cultural Heritage', J Paul Getty Trust Occasional Papers in Cultural Heritage Policy, Number 2 (2018).

Roger Matthews, Qais Hussain Rashees, Mónica Palmero Fernández, Seán Fobbe, Karel Nováček, Rozhen Mohammed-Amin, Simone Mühl and Amy Richardson, 'Heritage and Cultural Healing: Iraq in a post-Daesh era' (2019) *International Journal of Heritage Studies* https://doi.org/10.1080/13527258.2019.1608585 accessed 10 November 2019.

Theodor Meron, 'The Protection of Cultural Property in the Event of Armed Conflict within the Case-law of the International Criminal Tribunal for the Former Yugoslavia' (2005) 57(4) *Museum International* 41.

Lynn Meskell, *A Future in Ruins* (Oxford University Press 2018).

Minority Rights Group, 'Protecting the Right to Culture for Minorities and Indigenous Peoples: An Overview of International Case Law', *State of the World's Minorities and Indigenous Peoples 2016* (Minority Rights Group 2016).

'"Monuments Men": New Army Unit to Protect Ancient Treasures', *Forces Network*(31 January 2019), https://www.forces.net/news/military-wants-reservists-indiana-jones-flair-new-unit accessed 10 November 2019.

A Dirk Moses, 'Raphael Lemkin, Culture and the Concept of Genocide", in Donald Bloxham and A Dirk Moses (eds), *The Oxford Handbook of Genocide Studies* (Oxford University Press 2010).

James AR Nafziger, Robert Kirkwood Paterson and Alison Dundes Renteln (eds), *Cultural Law* (Cambridge University Press 2010).

NATO, *The Protection of Cultural Property in the Event of Armed Conflict: Unnecessary Distraction or Mission Relevant Priority?* (NATO OPEN Publications 2018).

C Nordstrom 'Terror Warfare and the Medicine of Peace' (1998) 12(1) *Medical Anthropology Quarterly* 103.

Elise Novic, *The Concept of Cultural Genocide* (Oxford University Press 2016).

Roger O'Keefe, *The Protection of Cultural Property during Armed Conflict* (Cambridge University Press 2006).

See V Pavone, *From the Labyrinth of the World to the Paradise of the Heart: Science and Humanism* (Lexington Books 2008).

Bibliography 97

Jadranka Petrovic, 'The Cultural Dimension of Peace Operations: Peacekeeping and Cultural Property', in Andrew H Campbell (ed), *Global Leadership Initiatives for Conflict Resolution and Peacebuilding* (IGI Global 2018).

Polybius, trans by Robin Waterfield, *Book IX: The Histories* (Oxford University Press 2010). See also, US Committee of the Blue Shield, 'History of Protection of Cultural Property: Ancient Authors' https://uscbs.org/antiquity.html accessed 10 November 2019.

Lyndel V Prott and Patrick J O'Keefe, '"Cultural Heritage' or 'Cultural Property"?' (1992) 1 *International Journal of Cultural Property* 307.

David Rieff, 'REP, RIP', *New York Times*, 7 November 2011, http://www.nytimes.com/2011/11/08/opinion/r2p-rip.html.

William Schabas, 'Preface' in Raphael Lemkin, *Axis Rule in Occupied Europe: Laws of Occupation-Analysis of Government-Proposals for Redress* (end edn, first published 1944, Lawbook Exchange, Ltd 2008).

Suzanne L Schairer, 'The Intersection of Human Rights and Cultural Property Issues under International Law' (2001) 11 *Italian Yearbook of International Law* 59.

Secretary General's address at event on 'Responsible Sovereignty: International Cooperation for a Changed World' (15 July 2008) https://www.un.org/sg/en/content/sg/statement/2008-07-15/secretary-generals-address-event-responsible-sovereignty.

Ralph Steinke, 'A Look Back at NATO's 1999 Kosovo Campaign: A Questionably "Legal" but Justifiable Exception?' (2015) 14(4) *Connections* 43.

Charlotte Steinorth, 'The Security Council's Response to the Ebola Crisis: A Step Forward or Backwards in the Realization of the Right to Health?' *EJIL: Talk!* (2 March 2017) https://www.ejiltalk.org/the-security-councils-response-to-the-ebola-crisis-a-step-forward-or-backwards-in-the-realization-of-the-right-to-health/ accessed 10 November 2019.

Jiri Toman, *The Protection of Cultural Property in the Event of Armed Conflict* (Dartmouth Publishing Company 1996).

UNESCO, 'Background note to the International Conference "Heritage and Cultural Diversity at Risk in Iraq and Syria" – The Protection of Heritage and Cultural Diversity: A Humanitarian and Security Imperative in the Conflicts of the 21st Century', UNESCO Headquarters, Paris, (3 December 2014).

UNESCO, *Report of the International Conference 'Heritage and Cultural Diversity at Risk in Iraq and Syria* (2014), p. 24 http://www.unesco.org/culture/pdf/iraq-syria/IraqSyriaReport-en.pdf accessed 10 November 2019.

UNESCO, *Report of the International Conference 'Heritage and Cultural Diversity at Risk in Iraq and Syria* (2014).

UNESCO, 'Strategy for the Reinforcement of UNESCO's Action for the Protection of Culture and the Promotion of Cultural Pluralism in the Event of Armed Conflict' (2015).

UNESCO, 'Italy Creates a UNESCO Emergency Task Force for Culture' (16 February 2016) http://whc.unesco.org/en/news/1436/ accessed 10 November 2019.

UNESCO, 'UNESCO Director-General: "Protecting Culture is a Moral Responsibility and a Security Issue"' (16 February 2016) http://www.unesco.or

Bibliography

g/new/en/media-services/single-view/news/unesco_director_general_protecting_culture_is_a_moral_resp/ accessed 10 November 2019.

UNESCO, 'International Criminal Court and UNESCO Strengthen Co-operation on the Protection of Cultural Heritage' (6 November 2017) https://en.unesco.org/news/international-criminal-court-and-unesco-strengthen-cooperation-protection-cultural-heritage accessed 10 November 2019.

UNESCO, 'The Director-General of UNESCO Calls for all Syrians to Commit to the Safeguarding of Cultural Heritage in Bosra and Idlib' (nd) http://whc.unesco.org/en/news/1257 accessed 10 November 2019.

UNESCO, 'UNESCO Director-General Condemns Destruction at Nimrud' (nd) http://en.unesco.org/news/unesco-director-general-condems-destruction-nimrud accessed 10 November 2019.

UNESCO, 'The Director-General of UNESCO Irina Bokova Calls on Iraqis to Stand United and Protect their Cultural Heritage' http://en.unesco.org/news/director-general-unesco-irina-bokova-calls-iraqis-stand-united-around-their-cultural-heritage.

UNESCO Heritage Centre, 'Interview with Peter King, Chair of the World Heritage Committee' (2001) May–June *World Heritage Newsletter* 2 http://whc.unesco.org/documents/publi_news_30_en.pdf accessed 10 November 2019.

United Nations Office on Genocide Prevention and the Responsibility to Protect, 'Responsibility to Protect' (nd) https://www.un.org/en/genocideprevention/about-responsibility-to-protect.shtml.

UN Secretary General, Press Release SG/SM/7136, 20 September 1999.

UN Secretary General Ban Ki-moon, in UNESCO, 'Background note to the International Conference "Heritage and Cultural Diversity at Risk in Iraq and Syria" – The Protection of Heritage and Cultural Diversity: A Humanitarian and Security Imperative in the Conflicts of the 21st Century', UNESCO Headquarters, Paris, (3 December 2014).

'US Army Creates Cultural Heritage Task Force', *Artforum* (22 October 2019) https://www.artforum.com/news/us-army-creates-cultural-heritage-task-force-81101 accessed 10 November 2019.

US Committee of the Blue Shield, 'History of Protection of Cultural Property: Ancient Authors' https://uscbs.org/antiquity.html accessed 10 November 2019. See also M Tullius Cicero, trans by CD Yonge, *The Orations of Marcus Tullius Cicero* (George Bel & Sons 1903).

Robert van Krieken, 'Cultural Genocide Reconsidered' (2008) 12 *Australian Indigenous Law Review* 76.

Emer de Vattel, edited and with Introduction by Béla Kapossy and Richard Whitmore, *The Law of Nations or the Principles of Natural Law Applied to the Conduct and to the Affairs of Nations and of Sovereigns* (Liberty Fund 2008), Book III, Chapter IX, §168.

Ana Filipa Vrdoljak, 'The Criminalisation of the Intentional Destruction of Cultural Heritage' in Tiffany Bergin and Emanuela Orlando (eds), *Forging a Socio-Legal Approach to Environmental Harms. Global Perspectives* (Routledge 2017), 237.

Ole Waever, 'Securitisation and Desecuritisation', in Ronnie D Lischutz (ed), *On Security* (Columbia University Press 1995), 46.

Helen Walasek et al., *Bosnia and the Destruction of Cultural Heritage* (Routledge 2016).

Thomas G Weiss and Nina Connelly, 'Cultural Cleansing and Mass Atrocities', J Paul Getty Trust Occasional Papers in Cultural Heritage Policy, Number 1 (2017).

Gary Wilson, 'Collective Security, "Threats to the Peace", and the Ebola Outbreak" (2015) 6(1) *Journal of Philosophy of International Law* 1.

Kristel Witkam, 'Cultural Property in Conflict', *Peace Palace Library Blog* 4 August 2016 https://www.peacepalacelibrary.nl/2016/08/cultural-property-in-co nflict/ accessed 10 November 2019.

Hikaru Yamashita, 'Reading "Threats to International Peace and Security" 1946–2005' (2007) 18(3) *Diplomacy & Statecraft* 551.

UN Reports

Ad Hoc Committee on Genocide, 'Report of the Committee and Draft Convention Drawn up by the Committee', (24 May 1948) UN ESCOR, UN Doc E/794.

ECOSOC, 'Ad Hoc Committee on Genocide: Summary Record of the Third Meeting', (16 April 1948) UN Doc E/AC.25/SR.5.

ECOSOC 'Two Hundred and Eighteenth Meeting: Draft Convention on the Crime of Genocide' (26 August 1948) E/SR.218.

High Level Panel Report on Threats, Challenges and Change, 'A more secure world: our shared responsibility', (2004) A/59/565.

Human Rights Council (17th Session) 'Report of Independent Expert in the Field of Cultural Rights, Farida Shaheed', (21 March 2011) A/HRC/17/38.

International Law Commission Report, *Yearbook of the International Law Commission* (1991), 268.

Office of the High Commissioner for Human Rights, 'The International Destruction of Cultural Heritage as a Violation of Human Rights', Report of the Special Rapporteur in the Field of Cultural Rights, Karima Bennoune, (9 August 2016) UN Doc A/71/317.

Report of the International Law Commission on the Work of its Forty-Eighth Session, UN Doc A/51/10, 90-1.

Report of the Secretary General, 'In Larger Freedom: Towards Development, Security and Human Rights for All', A/59/2005 https://undocs.org/A/59/2005.

Report of the Secretary General on the implementation of Security Council Resolution 2347.

Report of the Secretary General Pursuant to Paragraph 2 of Security Council Resolution 808 (1993), UN Doc S/25704, 12.

UNSC, 'Final Report of the Commission of Experts Established Pursuant to Security Council Resolution 780 (1992)' (27 May 1994) UN Doc S/1994/674.

UN Document, 'Report of the Secretary-General, Implementing the Responsibility to Protect', (12 January 2009) A/63/677.

World Summit Outcome Document, (2005) A/RES/60/1 https://www.un.org/en/development/desa/population/migration/generalassembly/docs/globalcompact/A_RES_60_1.pdf.

Legal Instruments

Instructions for the Government of Armies of the United States in the Field. Prepared by Francis Lieber, promulgated as General Orders No. 100 by President Lincoln, 24 April 1863.

Project of an International Declaration concerning the Laws and Customs of War, signed at Brussels, 27 August 1874.

The Laws of War on Land, Manual published by the Institute of International Law (Oxford Manual), adopted by the Institute of International Law at Oxford, September 9, 1880.

Hague Convention II with Respect to the Laws and Customs of War on Land and its annex: Regulation concerning the Laws and Customs of War on Land, 1899.

Hague Convention IV with Respect to the Laws and Customs of War on Land, 1907 and Article 5 of Hague Convention IX concerning Bombardment by Naval Forces in Time of War, 1907.

Roerich Pact, signed in the White House, in the presence of President Franklin Delano Roosevelt, on 15 April 1935.

Agreement by the Government of the United Kingdom of Great Britain and Northern Ireland, the Government of the United States of America, the Provisional Government of the French Republic and the Government of the Union of Soviet Socialist Republics for the Prosecution and Punishment of the Major War Criminal of the European Axis, 82 UNTS 279, signed and entered into force 8 August 1945.

Charter of the International Military Tribunal – Annex to the Agreement for the prosecution and punishment of the major war criminals of the European Axis ('London Agreement'), August 8, 1945, 82 UNTC, 280.

Control Council Order No 10: Punishment of Persons Guilty of War Crimes, Crimes against Peace and against Humanity, 20 December 1945, (1946) 3 *Official Gazette Control Council for Germany* 50.

Convention on the Prevention and Punishment of the Crime of Genocide, opened for signature 9 December 1948, 78 UNTS 277.

Universal Declaration of Human Rights, proclaimed by the United Nations General Assembly in Paris on 10 December 1948 (General Assembly resolution 217 A).

Geneva Convention for the Amelioration of the Condition of the Wounded and Sick in Armed Forces in the Field (First Geneva Convention), adopted 12 August 1949.

Geneva Convention for the Amelioration of the Condition of Wounded, Sick and Shipwrecked Members of Armed Forces at Sea (Second Geneva Convention), adopted 12 August 1949.

Geneva Convention relative to the Treatment of Prisoners of War (Third Geneva Convention), adopted 12 August 1949.

Geneva Convention Relative to the Protection of Civilian Persons in Time of War (Fourth Geneva Convention), adopted 12 August 1949.

Convention for the Protection of Cultural Property in the Event of Armed Conflict, adopted at The Hague, 1954, 249 UNTS 240.

First Protocol to the Convention for the Protection of Cultural Property in the Event of Armed Conflict 1954, adopted at The Hague, 14 May 1954, 249 UNTS 358.

Bibliography 101

International Covenant on Civil and Political Rights, adopted by the General Assembly of the United Nations on 19 December 1966, 999 UNTS 171.

UNESCO Convention on the Means of Prohibiting and Preventing the Illicit Import, Export and Transfer of Ownership of Cultural Property, adopted at Paris, 14 November 1970, 823 UNTS 231.

World Heritage Convention Concerning the Protection of the World Cultural and Natural Heritage, adopted at Paris, 16 November 1972.

Protocol Additional to the Geneva Conventions of 12 August 1949, and relating to the Protection of Victims of International Armed Conflicts (Protocol I), 8 June 1977.

Protocol Additional to the Geneva Conventions of 12 August 1949, and relating to the Protection of Victims of Non-International Armed Conflicts (Protocol II), 8 June 1977.

Statute of the International Criminal Tribunal of the Former Yugoslavia as established by Security Council Resolution 827 (1993).

Statute of the International Criminal Tribunal for Rwanda as established by Security Council Resolution 955 (1994).

Statute of the International Criminal Court (1998), 2187 UNTS 90.

Second Protocol to the Convention for the Protection of Cultural Property in the Event of Armed Conflict 1954, adopted at The Hague, 26 March 1999, 2252 UNTS 172.

Statute of the Special Court for Sierra Leone as established pursuant to Security Council Resolution 1315 (2000).

Agreement between the Government of the State of Eritrea and the Government of the Federal Democratic Republic of Ethiopia (signed 12 December 2000, entered into force on the date of signature) UN Doc A/55/686-S/2000/1183 Annex

Law on the Establishment of the Extraordinary Chambers in the Courts of Cambodia for the Prosecution of Crimes Committed During the Period of Democratic Kampuchea (2001) (Cambodia).

Convention for the Safeguarding of the Intangible Cultural Heritage, adopted at Paris, 17 October 2003.

UNESCO Declaration concerning the Intentional Destruction of Cultural Heritage, adopted at Paris, 17 October 2003.

Convention on the Protection and Promotion of the Diversity of Cultural Expressions, adopted at Paris, 20 October 2005.

United Nations Declaration on the Rights of Indigenous Peoples, adopted by the General Assembly, 2 October 2007, A/RES/61/295.

Protocol on Restitution of Cultural Assets from Serbia to Croatia (signed 23 March 2012).

Abu Dhabi Declaration (3 December 2016).

Memorandum of Understanding between the United Nations Educational, Scientific and Cultural Organization and the ICRC (2016).

Convention on Offences relating to Cultural Property, Council of Europe Treaty Series No 221 (2017).

Caselaw

International Military Tribunal

France and ors v Göring (Hermann) and ors, Judgment and Sentence, [1946] 22 IMT 203, (1946) 41 AJIL 172, (1946) 13 ILR 203, ICL 243 (IMTN 1946), 1st October 1946, International Military Tribunal, 248 and 302.

International Court of Justice

Application of the Convention on the Prevention and Punishment of the Crime of Genocide (Bosnia and Herzegovina v Serbia and Montenegro) (Merits) [2007] ICJ Rep 4.

Advisory Opinion, Reservations to the Convention on the Prevention and Punishment of the Crime of Genocide [1951] ICJ Rep 15.

ICTY

Prosecutor v Blaškic, IT-95-14, Trial Judgement, 3 March 2000.
Prosecutor v Kordić and Čerzek, IT-95-14/2-A, Trial Chamber Judgment, 26 February 2001.
Prosecutor v Kristić IT-98-33-T, Trial Chamber Judgment, 2 August 2001.

ICC

Prosecutor v Al Mahdi ICC-01/12-01/15.
Prosecutor v Al Hassan Ag Abdoul Aziz Ag Mohamed Ag Mahmoud ICC-01/12-01/18.

Inter-American Court of Human Rights

Plan de Sánchez Massacre v Guatemala, Judgement (Reparations), 19 November 2004.
Yakye Axa Indigenous Community v Paraguay, Judgment (Merits, Reparations and Costs), 17 June 2005.

UN Security Council Resolutions

SC Res 1973 (March 17, 2011).
SC Res 2347 (24 March 2017).
SC Res 1267 (15 October 1999).
SC Res 1483 (22 May 2003).
SC Res 2056 (5 July 2012).
SC Res 2085 (20 December 2012).
SC Res 2100 (25 April 2013).
SC Res 2139 (22 February 2014).

SC Res 1483 (22 May 2003).
SC Res 1267 (1999).
SC Res 2199 (12 February 2015).
SC Res 2347 (24 March 2017).
SC Resolution 2170 (15 August 2014).
SC Resolution 2347 (24 March 2017).
SC Resolution 2100 (25 April 2013).
SC Resolution 2295 (29 June 2016).
SC Resolution 2480 (28 June 2019).
SC Resolution 2347 (24 March 2017).
SC Resolution 2177 (18 September 2014).

General Assembly Resolutions

GA Res 96(I), UN GAOR, 1st sess, 55th mtg, UN Doc A/ES/96(I), (11 December, 1946).
GA Resolution 60/1, UN Doc A/RES/60/1 (24 October, 2005),
GA Res 67/929-S/2013/399 (July 9, 2013).
GA Res 70/999-S/2016/620 (August 17, 2016).
GA Res 70/1 (21 October 2015).
GA Res 69/281 (28 May 2015).

Index

2030 Agenda for Sustainable
    Development 84

Abu Dhabi Declaration on
    Safeguarding Endangered Cultural
    Heritage (2016) 68–69
Afghanistan 9, 63–64, 92
Africa 3, 36–38, 47, 60
African Charter on Human and
    Peoples' Rights 3
African Commission on Human and
    Peoples' Rights 3
African Union 45
Al Qaeda in the Islamic Maghreb
    (AQIM) 27, 74
Alexander II of Russia 12
American Academy of Arts and
    Sciences 43
Annan, K. 40
Ansar Dine 1, 9, 27–29, 32, 36,
    73, 74
Arab Legion 8

Balkan Wars 8, 25, 39, 47, 52
Balta, A. 30
Bamiyan Buddha statues 9, 24
Ban Ki-moon 43, 46, 83
barbarity 3, 48, 79
Benin 45
Bensouda, F. 71
Blue Helmets for Culture 72, 81
Boko Haram 45
Bokova, I. 5, 36–38, 44, 62, 71,
    82–83, 89
British Institute of International and
    Comparative Law 77, 83

Cairo 92
Cameroon 45
Campbell, A. 61
Carthage 10
Chad 45
Cicero, M. T. 10, 16
civil society 43, 46, 61, 65
clash of civilizations 80
Cold War 38; post- 1
collateral damage 1, 4, 25, 36
Commission on Responsibility
    of the Authors of the War and on
    Enforcement of Penalties (1919) 15
Convention for the Safeguarding of the
    Intangible Cultural Heritage (2003) 18
Convention on Cultural Property
    (1954) 20
Convention on the Protection and
    Promotion of the Diversity of
    Cultural Expressions (2005) 18
Copenhagen School 62
Council of Europe Convention on
    Offences relating to Cultural
    Property (2017) 71
crimes against culture 10, 22, 33, 91
criminal responsibility 4, 10, 22, 24,
    25, 57, 89
Croatia 34
cultural: activities 49; artefacts 64,
    70, 88; assets 34; awareness 77;
    bodies 51; characteristics 53;
    cleansing 1, 5, 7, 35–39, 44, 46–47,
    58–60, 62; destruction 49, 58–59, 85;
    development 61, 68, 72; diversity 3,
    37, 61, 67, 72, 81, 85; engineering
    37; exchanges 18; genocide 5, 7,

Index 105

20, 35, 38, 44, 47–59; goods 11, 68; identity 6, 19, 25, 53, 85; institutions 50, 53, 71; issue 66; items 16–17; life 17, 20, 29; objects 26, 32, 71, 77; peacekeeping 6, 61–63, 72, 75, 77, 80, 83; perspective 76; preservation 75; property 5–6, 11, 15–18, 22–23, 25, 27, 36, 38, 44, 54–55, 61, 65, 67–69, 71, 73–74, 76–78, 80, 83, 85; protection 74–75, 78–79, 81, 85; representations 2; rights 19–20, 72, 88; significance 37, 63; sites 1, 4, 8–9, 25, 37–38, 63, 66, 75, 87; values 56; warfare 5
Cultural Heritage Task Force 82
Cultural Property Protection Unit 82
Cuno, J. 35, 43, 92

Da'esh *see* Islamic State in Iraq and the Levant
de Vattel, E. 11, 16, 87
Declaration of Brussels (1874) 11
destruction 3–4, 7, 10, 13–16, 19, 22, 24–33, 35–38, 43–45, 47–48, 50–51, 53–54, 58–59, 61–63, 65–69, 71–73, 75, 81, 84–85, 87, 89–92; acts of 3; biological 53–55; deliberate 1, 8, 54; general 4; impact of 30; intentional 1, 24, 71–72; malicious 48; material 52; of monuments 37; of personal security 49; physical 50, 54–55; systematic 4, 50; targeted 65; unlawful 67; wanton 15, 23, 25; weapons of mass 66; *see also* cultural
Dirk Moses, A. 49
diversity 85; destruction of 37; elimination of 2; rich 37; *see also* cultural
Draft Code of Crimes 52

Eakin, H. 43
Ebola crisis 84
economic: developments 61, 68, 70, 72; existence 49; loss 30; regeneration 83; security 83; terms 80; vitality 61
education 12–15, 17, 21–22, 25–27, 61, 65, 76, 80, 88
Emergency Safeguarding of the Syrian Heritage Project 75

Eritrea-Ethiopia Claims Commission 34
ethnic cleansing 38–41, 44, 90
European Union Delegation to the UN 60
extremism 37, 65, 79

Fifth International Conference for the Unification of Criminal Law 48
Florence Declaration (2017) 70
Foradori, P. 2, 4, 62, 76–78, 83, 85
France 45
Frulli, M. 5, 19, 21, 88
fundamentalist Islamic groups 1, 28, 36, 80, 87, 89

Geneva Conventions (1949) 17, 72
genocide 20, 26–27, 32–33, 39–41, 44, 47–57, 90; acts of 41, 44, 48, 50–51, 54, 56; Ad Hoc Committee on Genocide 53; Application of the Genocide Convention 54; Armenian 48; biological 49, 53; claims of 52; conception of 52, 56, 58; crime of 38, 43–44, 47–48, 50, 53, 57, 90; intent to commit 26, 38; physical 53; situations of 47; state-sponsored 56; technique of 48; *see also* cultural
Genocide Convention (1948) 20, 47, 50, 52–58, 90
Ghaddafi, M. 42
Global Centre for the Responsibility to Protect 60
Grotius, H. 10, 87

Hague Convention for the Protection of Cultural Property in the Event of Armed Conflict (1954) 4, 15–16, 19, 23, 34–35, 72, 75, 88
Hague Conventions on the Laws and Customs of War (1899 and 1907) 9, 11–12, 14, 19, 22, 87, 88
Hague Peace Conference (1899) 14
Heine, H. 49
heritage 6, 10, 19, 29, 34, 64, 67, 70, 77, 80, 87, 91–92; attacks on 89; common 24; destruction of 47, 58; historical 54, 63; importance 32; issues 88; local 76; multiple 21; natural 18; protection of 46; religious

54, 63; shared 77; sites 1, 77–78; value of 32
High Level Panel on Threats, Challenges and Change 40
Hisbah 27
historical: importance 64; monuments 50, 53; roots 61, 67, 72; sites 63, 73, 75; value 50; *see also* heritage
HIV/AIDS 43
Holocaust 48–50
human rights 3, 19–21, 37, 52, 61; abuses of 65; discourse 88; law 21, 31; monitoring of 73; treaties 20; violation of 21, 40

iconoclasm 1, 9, 62
identity 2, 21, 37, 39, 44, 53–54, 62, 83, 87, 92; aspect of 37; collective 61; of communities 89, 91; group 2, 26, 32, 37–38; marker 10; people's 38; religious 26; shared 16; societal 84; symbol of 25; wars 1; *see also* cultural
indigenous peoples 19, 47, 52, 55–57
Institute of International Law 13
Inter-American Court of Human Rights 31
International Commission on Intervention and State Sovereignty (ICISS) 40–41, 46
International Committee of the Red Cross 70–71
International Council of Museums Emergency Red List of Syrian Cultural Objects at Risk 75
International Court of Justice (ICJ) 26, 54
International Covenant on Civil and Political Rights 20
International Covenant on Economic, Social and Cultural Rights (1966) 20
International Criminal Court (ICC) 4, 10, 27, 29, 32–33, 38, 47, 53, 71, 74, 89; Office of the Prosecutor Strategic Plan (2019–2021) 71; Rome Statute 10, 53
International Criminal Tribunal for the Former Yugoslavia (ICTY) 25–27, 32–33, 38, 52, 54, 89, 91
International Criminal Tribunal for Rwanda (ICTR) 52

International Law Commission 26, 45, 52–53, 91
International Military Tribunal 26; Nuremberg 23
international peace and security 6, 60, 62, 65–68, 74, 91
Interpol 64–65, 68
Iraq 1, 3, 5, 33–38, 63–65, 78–79, 83, 87; National Library 64; National Museum 64; War 76
Islamic: empire 3; fundamentalist groups 1, 36, 80, 87; leaders 28; police 32
Islamic State in Iraq and the Levant (ISIL) 65
Islamic State of Iraq and Syria (ISIS) 1, 34, 36, 45, 89
Italian Carabinieri Command for the Protection of Cultural Heritage 82

J Paul Getty Trust 43, 46
Jakubowski, A. 32, 67, 69, 81
Jerusalem 8

Kabul Museum 92
Karlsrud, J. 74
Keitel, W. 23
Kerry, J. 3

law: conventional 22; criminal 47, 70; cultural heritage 17, 70; customary 14, 21, 52, 54; domestic 64; humanitarian 3, 15, 21, 35, 45, 47, 65, 70, 88; human rights 21, 31; international 5, 11, 16, 21–22, 24–25, 33, 47, 50, 53, 55, 67, 70, 87; rule of 61; violations of 25; of war 12, 14
League of Nations 48
Lemkin, R. 48–52, 58, 90
Lenzerini, F. 9, 44–45
libraries 12, 50, 53, 63–64, 71, 73
Libya 1, 42, 47, 92
Lieber Code 12; (1863) 11; (1883) 87
Lincoln, A. 12
Lostal, M. 22–25, 34
Luck, E. C. 4, 33, 42, 45, 47, 55, 57, 61–63

Mali 1, 4, 9, 27–34, 45, 63, 73, 75, 87
Manual of the Laws and Customs of War at Oxford (1880) 11, 13–14

Matsuura, K. 25
Middle East 1, 36–38, 47, 59–60, 65, 87, 89, 92
minorities 20; linguistic 20; rights of 52
monuments 1, 11, 29, 35, 37, 63, 87; destruction of 37; historical 13–15, 21–22, 25, 27, 32, 50, 53; religious 50
mosques 8, 26–27, 30, 54
Movement for Unity and Jihad in West Africa (MUJAO) 74
Multinational Joint Task Force 45
museums 12, 50, 53, 63–64, 71, 87–88, 92
Muslim; non- 9; religion 26; saints 3

National Movement for the Liberation of Azawad (MNLA) 74
National Museum of Afghanistan 92
Niger 45
non-governmental organisation (NGO) 60
Nordstrom, C. 39
North Africa 1, 59, 87, 89, 92
North Atlantic Treaty Organization (NATO) 39, 42
Novic, E. 51–52, 55

paradigm 5, 7, 15, 35, 57–59, 87, 89–90; civilian use 5, 19, 27, 35, 88–89; cultural cleansing 60; cultural genocide 5, 47–48, 58; cultural heritage 70; cultural peacekeeping 76; cultural rights 88; culture-value 5, 19, 22, 35, 60, 89; divergent 11; effective 47, 89, 91–92; potential 90; protective 58; security 6–7, 59, 61, 85, 91; traditional 10
Paris Peace Conference 15
peace: framework 75, 85; global 70; operations 74, 76; resolution 73; and security 6, 56, 59–63, 65–68, 72, 74, 84–85, 91
peacebuilding 63, 73, 83; initiatives 6, 61; processes 81
peacekeeping 61, 72–73, 76–78, 80, 82; activities 81; forces 78; initiatives 80; light 78; mandates 73, 76, 78, 80–81; missions 62, 73–80, 83; operations 75; processes 81; realm 72; *see also* cultural

Permanent Mission of Italy to the UN 60
Petrovic, J. 5–6, 38, 73, 76–77
pillage 14
pluralism 2, 37, 85
Polybius 10
Prosecutor v Al Hassan 32
Prosecutor v Al Mahdi 4, 27–33, 74; Reparations Order 30–31
Prosecutor v Kordić and Čerzek 25
Prosecutor v Kristić 26, 53–55
Protecting Cultural Heritage from Terrorism and Mass Atrocities: Links and Common Responsibilities 60

reconciliation 3, 61, 68, 73, 84–85
Reichsleiter Rosenberg Taskforce 23
religious: activities 49; buildings 8, 15, 26, 29; connection 30; culture 26; element 53; ground 65; group 48, 50, 57; heritage 54, 63; identity 26, 53; importance 64; minorities 20; monuments 27, 50; presence 54; property 54–55; sites 15, 25, 27–28, 63, 65, 71; sources 28; value 50; worship 50
Responsibility to Protect (R2P) 5, 7, 35, 38–47, 58, 75, 83, 89–90
Rome Statute 10, 27, 32–33, 53, 71, 91
Rosenberg, A. 23

Schabas, W. 51
Scipio Aemilianus 10
Second International Peace Conference (1907) 14
securitisation 62, 65, 85; model 62; of cultural heritage 61–63, 70, 74, 83; state of 62
Serbia 34, 39
Shaheed, F. 21
Sheik Abdoul Kassim Attouaty Mausoleum 28
Sheik Mouhamad El Mikki Mausoleum 28
Sheik Sidi Ahmed Ben Amar Arragadi Mausoleum 28
Sheik Sidi El Mokhtar Ben Sidi Mouhammad Al Kabir Al Kounti Mausoleum 28
Sheikh Mohamed Mahmoud Al Arawani Mausoleum 28

108 *Index*

Sidi Mahamoud Ben Omar Mohamed Aquit Mausoleum 28
Sidi Yahia Mosque 28, 30
Smith, L. 74
Statute of the International Criminal Court 47
Statute of the International Criminal Tribunal for the Former Yugoslavia (ICTY) 25
Stolen Generations 56–57
sustainable development 83–84
Syracuse: Roman defeat of 10
Syria 1, 3, 5, 33–38, 45, 63–65, 78–79, 87, 89, 91
Syrian Antiquities Law (1963) 91

Taliban 9, 64
Temple of Serapis, Alexandria, Egypt 8
Theodosius 8
Timbuktu 3, 9, 27, 29–31, 63
trafficking 64–66, 68, 70; illicit 69, 71
Tripoli 92
Tuareg 27

UNIDROIT Convention on Stolen or Illegally Exported Cultural Objects (1995) 18, 91
United Nations (UN) 6, 20–21, 39–41, 43–45, 47, 50, 52, 57, 59–63, 65–67, 69, 72–75, 79, 84–85, 91
United Nations Declaration on the Right of Indigenous Peoples (UNDRIP) 55–56
United Nations Educational, Scientific and Cultural Organization (UNESCO) 1–2, 24, 30–31, 35–36, 38, 43, 58, 60, 62, 64–65, 68–71, 73, 81–82, 84–85, 88–89, 91; #Unite4Heritage campaign 69; Action for the Protection of Culture and the Promotion of Cultural Pluralism in the Event of Armed Conflict 81, 85; Conference for the Establishment of 61; Convention Concerning the Protection of the World Cultural and Natural Heritage 16; Convention for the Safeguarding of the Intangible Cultural Heritage 18; Convention on the Means of Prohibiting and Preventing the Illicit Import, Export and Transfer of Ownership of Cultural Property 16–17; Convention on the Protection and Promotion of the Diversity of Cultural Expressions 18; Convention on the Protection of the World Cultural and Natural Heritage 29; Declaration concerning the Intentional Destruction of Cultural Heritage (2003) 24, 72; World Heritage List 27; World Heritage Sites 27, 63
United Nations Multidimensional Integrated Stabilization Mission in Mali (MINUSMA) 73–75, 79, 81–82
United Nations Office on Drugs and Crime (UNODC) 60, 68–69
United Nations Security Council (UNSC) 63, 65, 67, 69, 73, 91; United Nations Permanent Five 62
United Nations World Summit meeting (2005) 41, 46
Universal Declaration of Human Rights (UDHR) 20, 51–52, 88

van Krieken, R. 57

war crime 15, 22–23, 27, 32, 38, 40–41, 44, 89–90
Weiss, T. G. 46
Wilson, P. 66
Witkam, K. 76
World War I 15
World War II 20, 23, 50, 88
World Customs Organization 68–69
World Heritage Convention Concerning the Protection of the World Cultural and Natural Heritage (1972) 18–19, 24–25, 89, 91
World Summit Outcome Document 41

year zero 2
Yemen 1, 34
Yugoslavia (former) 1, 25–26, 34, 38–39, 89